the
te

hire
Council
es

CRIMES

Also by Alberto Barerra Tyszka in English translation

The Sickness (2010)

ALBERTO BARRERA TYSZKA

CRIMES

Translated from the Spanish by
Margaret Jull Costa

MACLEHOSE PRESS
QUERCUS · LONDON

First published in Spanish as *Crímines* by
Editorial Anagrama, Barcelona, 2009
First published in Great Britain in 2015 by

MacLehose Press
An imprint of Quercus Publishing Ltd
Carmelite House
50 Victoria Embankment
London EC4Y 0DZ

An Hachette UK company

ISBN (HB) 978 0 85705 315 2
ISBN (Ebook) 978 1 84866 475 3

Contents

Nothing

FOR JUAN VILLORO

When they got up that morning, they found four drops of blood on the carpet.

Silvia was the first to notice. Women are always more observant than men. She emerged from the bedroom half-asleep, still brushing her teeth and still in the grey cotton shorts she sometimes wore in bed. The hair on the right-hand side of her head was sticking up as if she had just received an electric shock. The other half was flattened from being pressed against the pillow. She was probably en route to the kitchen to put the coffee on, when she stopped abruptly. She crouched down and scrutinised the carpet. No, she didn't just scrutinise it, she actually sniffed it.

"Rafael," she called, her eyes still glued to the floor, "come here!"

Her husband took his time. Silvia was rooted to the spot, still awkwardly clutching her now redundant toothbrush. The toothpaste in her mouth was fast losing its flavour and turning into a disagreeable froth. When Rafael finally appeared, holding the newspaper, she merely pointed at the floor before racing off to the bathroom to spit vigorously into the sink. She returned at once. Rafael was on all fours, studying the carpet.

"It's blood, isn't it?"

"Looks like it, yes. But it's dry."

"So? What does that mean?"

"How should I know?" Rafael accompanied this rather tetchy response with a gesture. "I suppose it means that it's not recent."

"But it's still blood. And how did a drop of blood manage to appear overnight?"

It wasn't just *one* drop of blood. In the living room, near the front door, they found another. Bewildered and with a growing sense of urgency, they started looking for more. She stumbled upon the third one just outside the kitchen. "Stumble upon" is not perhaps the most appropriate expression to use, but when she saw it, Silvia did stumble. As if she had bumped into the air, as if the small, round stain had its own invisible skeleton. Then she saw the fourth drop of blood, right next to the green three-seater sofa, close to the balcony. Silvia and Rafael looked at each other, nonplussed. With a slight grimace of disgust, Silvia watched Rafael reach out and touch the stain with the tip of his little finger. It wasn't dry but slightly viscous. It seemed quite fresh. A dark red sliver remained stuck to his nail. He held it to his nose and sniffed. "It doesn't smell of anything," he said.

They quickly deduced that the blood must have come from Sócrates. The cat was lying asleep in the magazine basket, shamelessly at ease. He was a large, hairy, neutered, bored creature. Not even bothering to wake the cat, Rafael picked him up and carried him over to the table, where they both carefully examined him.

They parted his fur, looking for some cut or wound; they lifted up his tail; they studied him from every possible angle. They found nothing to indicate that Sócrates had anything to do with those bloodstains. "But there's no other possible explanation," Silvia said, still ruffling the cat's fur. "Where else could the blood have come from?" Rafael glanced over at a lamp, a very male glance, imbued with a certain degree of mechanical knowledge. "Perhaps it's just grease or rust," he said, ready to develop a theory about how objects sweat, about the fluid nature of time. "Perhaps he's peeing or shitting blood," she said.

They went to the vet's together. It was Saturday. The vet on duty had warned them over the phone that they would have to pay extra: emergency consultations were not free. While they were driving there, Rafael was thinking that this whole affair could prove very expensive. He looked at Sócrates sitting calmly on his wife's lap. The cat was purring. He actually had the nerve to purr. "Cats purr when they're nervous too," his wife always said. She didn't say it then, but there was no need: the words were there, waiting in the wings. They could be spoken at any moment. Silvia was staring out of the window. She appeared to be deep in thought, as if she and her thoughts were elsewhere.

"What are you thinking about?"

Silvia merely shook her head.

Rafael knew she was thinking about something, but clearly didn't want to say what it was. Rafael knew, too, that it would be pointless to insist. They went through three more sets of lights in complete silence.

"You're annoyed, aren't you?" Silvia said, shooting him a reproachful look.

"Well, taking the cat to the vet's on a Saturday isn't exactly my idea of fun."

She turned towards the window again. She screwed up her eyes as if straining to see the empty streets.

The vet stuck a small tube up Sócrates' anus and pressed on his bladder. The cat didn't even miaow. He put up with this humiliation with lofty indifference. He released all the liquid inside him without a murmur, as if this were an entirely routine procedure he'd been having every week for years. The vet did several tests on his urine, but found no trace of blood. Nothing. Sócrates was perfectly healthy. He didn't even need his claws clipping. When the time came to pay, the cat lay on the counter wearing a rather bored expression, as if boredom were another form of revenge.

On the way home, Silvia and Rafael talked about bats.

A few months before, a couple of bats had taken to roosting just outside their bedroom window. The cleaning lady found them. Her name is Nereida and she comes every Tuesday. Silvia had asked her to clean the windows. As soon as she opened the window, though, Nereida let out a shriek of alarm. Those two hanging figures reminded her of gargoyles. Outside lurked an invisible cathedral that changed every night into a horrible grimace, a danger, an evil omen. Nereida started back. "Best just leave it be, *señora*," she said.

The bats hung in that dark corner of the eaves during the

day, but at night they were rarely there. Silvia and Rafael began observing them, though without ever opening the window. "They're disgusting," she used to say. "Not really," he would say, even though he found them equally disgusting. He felt that these strange hybrids – half-rodent, half-bird – had ended up with the worst qualities of both species. They were somehow unfinished, hopeless. Silvia and Rafael felt the same fear, the same repugnance, but neither of them knew how to solve the problem. Neither of them dared to confront the bats. They preferred to ignore them. To coexist peacefully, on the tacit understanding that some stable relationships survive only out of fear.

One afternoon, Silvia's brother Tomás arrived, carrying a small rifle. He opened the window and fired a shot into the corner. Just like that. Silvia immediately closed the window, then closed the curtains too. They didn't hear a sound. No scream. Nothing. They waited a few minutes. When they looked, there was nothing, only a dark stain on the wall.

Downstairs, in the inner courtyard, they found the mangled body of one of the bats. Silvia didn't even want to look. As well as being shot, the creature had fallen all the way from the second floor onto the tarmac. "What a mess," muttered her brother. She simply handed him a black plastic bag and a small shovel. All crimes create the same problem: what to do with the remains.

That night, when Rafael came home from work, Silvia was sitting on the bed, folding up the clothes she had just taken out of the dryer. She felt guilty. She was wondering, too, which of the bats had survived, the male or the female. She felt depressed. She was convinced that the surviving bat would come back, that sooner or later it would return to punish them. Rafael found all this highly amusing. He couldn't stop laughing. "Vampires are dangerous creatures," she said. "Yes, but we live in Latin America," he said, stroking her back. Then she made some comment about animals and geography. "We don't have vampires here, just bats," he said. And he kissed her. Silvia returned his kiss. Then she put her arms around him and held him close. She started touching him. Almost frenziedly. She unzipped his flies, knelt down before him and sucked his cock. They made love quickly, violently. With the curtains closed.

As soon as they walked into the apartment, she said just two words: "It's back." This, she felt, was the natural conclusion to the conversation they'd had on the journey home. If Sócrates was fine, then there could be no other explanation. What she feared had come true: the bat had returned. That was the origin of the drops of blood on the carpet. While they were still in the kitchen making coffee, they continued their discussion.

"It's the vampire or vampiress that didn't die. It's come back and got into the house, looking for its mate. It's here."

"That's just not possible."

"Why not?" Silvia suddenly glanced up at the ceiling. "They say that the things we remember best are the things we hate."

Rafael unconsciously followed the direction of his wife's eyes and stood staring at the ceiling for a few moments.

"All animals are vengeful," she said.

The water in the coffee-maker began to boil.

That afternoon, Rafael went to visit his parents. It was a routine he had kept up for years, every Saturday. He would put on his sports gear, as if the visit would demand some special physical effort from him. When they were first married, Silvia would sometimes go with him. Every other Saturday. But the years spent together have put paid to such niceties and they have developed a kind of division of labour, saving affection for those occasions when it is really necessary, thus making of their marriage an ever more efficient machine.

They had first met at a party given by Elena, Silvia's cousin. One of those dimly lit, alcohol-fuelled affairs. Elena had met Rafael by chance, through a mutual friend. She had immediately felt attracted to him, but, not wishing to appear too keen, had suggested to their friend that he invite Rafael to the party too. Silvia arrived later with her then boyfriend, who was of Italian stock: a strong, pale-skinned guy with a slow, easy smile. Everything about him was big, apart from his hands. These were so thin and bony they seemed like a mistake, as if they belonged to another body, as if he had stolen them from someone else. His name was Enzo. Silvia introduced him to Elena. And Elena, in turn, introduced her to Rafael, shooting Silvia a meaningful look, as if they had already discussed both these guys and were now assessing them visually. This proved fatal. Silvia and Rafael fell for each other almost instantaneously, the moment their eyes met. And it proved very hard to disguise those feelings of attraction.

From that point on, the party became a strange, almost pleasurable torture. Rafael could not stop staring at Silvia. She felt uncomfortable with Enzo by her side, but could not control the longing inside her, the glad, troubling tingle that Rafael's eyes provoked in her. Neither of them had ever experienced such a wild, animal chemistry before. Rafael left the party before a sixth glass of wine prompted him to do something foolish. He left without saying goodbye. Silvia and Enzo quarrelled and, fifteen minutes later, they too left the party, still quarrelling.

The following day, Rafael phoned her. He had persuaded his friend to get Elena to tell him Silvia's number. When Silvia heard his voice and name, she turned bright red. She felt an intense heat under her skin, was at a loss for words. Rafael suggested they meet for coffee. She was speechless. Overwhelmed. "Hello?" he said again. Then she finally managed to speak. Yes, she said. And she clung on to that one word. Yes.

After coffee, they began to kiss. Passionately, madly. As if kisses were going out of fashion. Suddenly, almost brusquely, Silvia drew back, pushing him away.

"What's wrong?"

"I'm still going out with Enzo," she said. "I'm still his girl-friend."

Enzo was at a bowling alley with his friends. When Silvia got there and saw him in the distance, she knew it wasn't going to be easy. All her confidence melted away. Rafael was waiting for her outside. Silvia stopped and took a deep breath. She couldn't help wondering if she was doing the right thing. She was, after all, acting purely on impulse. She wasn't thinking clearly. These words were ringing in her head with each step she took, as she approached the lane where her boyfriend was playing. Do you really know him? Do you know who he is? Are you going to change your life, just like that, simply because you fancy a guy? What's wrong with you, Silvia? What kind of woman are you? These questions were punctuated by the sound of the balls thundering down the lanes and crashing into the wooden skittles.

"Silvia!" Enzo looked at her, surprised. He had just been about to roll his ball down the lane when she appeared. "What are *you* doing here?"

A strange, serious expression must have flickered across her face. Her boyfriend's friends stood up and they, too, stared at her in bewilderment.

"Can we talk?"

There is no right moment to say to someone: "I don't love you anymore." There is no ideal scenario. There are no kind words in which to wrap that stone before you throw it. Silvia would have preferred to phone him or send him a note. But that would have felt just as cowardly and disloyal. Now that he was there before her, she didn't know what to do, how to find the best way of letting him down. His friends, standing a little way away, were still staring at them.

"What's wrong, Silvia? Tell me."

She felt a thick ball of saliva forming on the tip of her tongue.

"I don't want to be your girlfriend anymore," she said. "I want us just to be good friends," she added, feeling increasingly nervous and uncomfortable. "I'm sorry." Enzo was still gazing at her in total confusion. "I'm really sorry." Enzo glanced at his friends out of the corner of his eye, then looked hard at Silvia. "God, I feel like a complete shit," she said before rushing off.

When she got out onto the pavement, her eyes were dazzled by the afternoon sun. She stopped. Blinked. Unable to hold back her tears. She searched for Rafael's car. Then she heard the plastic click-click of hurrying feet, heard her name. It was Enzo, vast and inconsolable. He had followed her. He was utterly confused. His bowling shoes were too big for him. The hire shop hadn't had his size. He came clicking over to her. Even though the shoes were more like flippers, at that moment his feet looked as small as his hands.

"I just don't understand, Silvia." He took a step nearer. Again the click of plastic on tarmac. "Please, don't leave me like this."

The green nose of Rafael's Chevrolet drew up alongside. Enzo stared at the car and at them. Silvia said something, although no-one can remember what. She jumped into the car. They drove off. In the rear-view mirror, they saw the vast figure of Enzo and saw that he did not go back into the bowling alley. Instead, he turned and crossed the road, taking very short steps.

Silvia and Rafael have been together ever since. Now, when they look back at the past, they sometimes wonder what happened to all that frenzy, all that mad passion. Obviously, they didn't expect it to last forever. Everyone knows that pleasure has an end. The senses grow old. They even talked about it once. She tended to believe that love comes in doses, that it can be weighed and measured. That they hadn't known how to administer it sensibly and had used it up far too quickly. Then all they had left was nostalgia. A tender nostalgia that helped them to stay together. What they loved most was what they had been. They had squandered the best part of their life together.

Rafael was of the view that their love had changed, that it now had other obsessions, weaknesses, other ways of expressing itself. Affections are like Heraclitus' river. No-one steps into the same affection twice. Their feelings for each other were the same, but different. That is what Rafael thought and said: "Perhaps not having children has affected us too."

After two years of marriage, Silvia became pregnant. Everything went perfectly normally. They kept strictly to the recommended routines. Silvia never overdid things. She didn't fall over or do anything foolish. She followed all the doctor's instructions to the letter. She even walked at least half a mile a day throughout her pregnancy. Rafael went with her. They were both so excited. The night Silvia's waters broke, they had everything ready. They knew it was going to happen one of these nights. They informed the doctor and their families, took their bag, already packed, and set off to the hospital. Silvia took a long time to dilate. Not even the injections they gave her helped. Her desire to give birth without any medical assistance crumpled in the face of the hospital doctors' advice. She was rushed into the operating theatre. They asked Rafael if he wanted to come too, but he preferred to stay outside. He had intended to be there at the birth and had even brought a video camera so as to capture the excitement of the moment, but the prospect of a Caesarean changed everything, it wasn't the same. He decided to wait in the corridor.

According to the medical report, the baby had the umbilical cord wrapped around its neck and there was nothing the doctors could do to save it. During the birth, the child was deprived of oxygen and suffered brain death. Rafael and Silvia were left feeling utterly empty. They couldn't find a single word to say, not so much as a monosyllable. They felt violated. They had been looted, plundered.

The hospital offered them a more detailed report. They produced the results of various examinations, laboratory tests, an autopsy. Some members of their family suggested suing the hospital for negligence, but neither Silvia nor Rafael wanted to investigate further. "Nothing will bring back our son," they said, or words to that effect. That's what people usually say in those circumstances. Rafael and Silvia could think of nothing else. All they felt was a great absence. The baby was a boy. He would have been called Gabriel.

When Silvia was discharged, and she and Rafael were leaving the hospital, the doctor accompanied them to the lift. Rafael and Silvia were still in shock.

"These things happen," he said. "It wasn't anyone's fault. It was a natural occurrence," he added awkwardly, his voice breaking. "Besides, you're still young. You have time."

Those words bounced back and forth between them. The months passed and still they didn't disappear. "It was a natural occurrence." The words were still there. They had a life of their own. They would turn up when least expected, springing out at them, regardless of place or circumstance. It was as though they had each swallowed a razor blade. As though that bright, shiny piece of metal could suddenly make itself felt, without warning, at any time. For example: Silvia in the shower, washing, touching herself with the small bar of soap. And suddenly she would feel a sharp pain inside. There was that huge razor blade standing upright in her vagina, even leaving a metallic taste on the back of her tongue. For example: Rafael on his way to work, stopping the car on a corner. A group of schoolboys walking to school. They're all dressed the same, but each one is different. They're laughing too loudly. The blade lies down behind his eyes. It transforms the horizon into an aluminium line that burns, that hurts. For example: the two of them together, having a late breakfast on a Sunday. Not saying a word.

Time, however, can soothe the most rancorous of feelings. They never wanted to try again. They didn't even talk about it. A silent pact was sealed between them. Silvia has continued to use various forms of contraception, and Rafael has never felt in the least surprised that she hasn't become pregnant again. They don't talk about it and if, by chance, the subject comes up at some social gathering, they simply avoid it. Then one Thursday in November, she came home with a kitten. "What do you think?" she asked.

When Rafael returned from visiting his parents, Silvia had already begun. "I can't stand it any longer," she said. She was barefoot, wearing a pair of brown shorts and a sleeveless white T-shirt. Her hair was caught back with an elastic band. She seemed restless, on edge. She had started with the living room and had already moved all the furniture out of the way, including the sofa and the two armchairs. The rugs had been rolled up and placed near the door to the balcony. She had even unzipped the covers of the sofa cushions and removed the foam filling. Not even the kitchen clock was in its usual place. The tall wooden cabinet where they kept the CD player was empty too, and the floor was littered with piles of CDs.

"I've been waiting for you," she said. "I need your help."

"This is crazy, Silvia."

"No, what's crazy is just sitting back and doing nothing."

"What do you expect to find? The bat?"

"Whatever. I don't care. But we need to know where those bloodstains are coming from."

They spent the afternoon meticulously searching the apartment. Inch by inch. They studied every bit of the ceiling. They shifted all the furniture, emptied all the drawers and wardrobes and, by six o'clock, they were exhausted. They sat on the floor for a few minutes, surveying everything they had managed to undo in that short space of time. It looked as if they were either moving house or had just moved in. Everything was scattered in disorderly fashion about the floor, including the cutlery from the kitchen. They had even taken down the two Paul Klee posters they had bought years ago from the local modern art museum. The house was a mess. The bloodstains were still there on the carpet.

That night, they drank whisky with water and went to bed without putting anything away. They were too tired. To reach their room, they had to skirt around boxes, suitcases and clothes. Silvia went to have a shower. When she came back, Rafael was lying on the bed, glass in hand, staring up at the ceiling.

"Can I turn out the light?"

Rafael nodded.

For a few minutes, they said nothing. Silvia lay down on her side, her back to him. Neither of them could sleep.

"I was thinking about Julio," Rafael said suddenly.

Julio is his best friend, they work at the same firm of architects. He's married and has a seven-year-old daughter.

"He's really worried about Marlene."

"What's wrong with her?"

"She keeps having nightmares."

Silvia turned over and looked at him. Rafael explained that the girl apparently wakes up each night, screaming in terror. When Julio goes in to her, he can do nothing to calm her. The girl cries and screams and thrashes about. He tries to reassure her, but she keeps crying, as if the dream had carried her off to some other place, to some prison from which she could never escape. One night, she dug her nails into Julio's arm. The marks stayed for a whole week: they looked like black lines cut into his skin. Julio feels powerless. He would like to take action, to shake her out of it, but he's been told that won't help. The girl seems completely sunk in herself, a prisoner of the dark, and yet she squeezes his hand really hard, too hard. She spends the night calling out to him to help her.

"What does she dream about? What kind of nightmare is it?"

"Julio doesn't know, but it must be something really horrible to cause such fear, such panic. Once, in the middle of one of these nightmares, she looked him in the eye and begged him: 'Save me, Papa, save me!' That's what Julio told me. Can you imagine?"

"Have they taken her to see a psychologist?"

"Yes."

"And?"

"He told them it was perfectly normal," Rafael said, after a pause.

But the idea of the girl suffering like that is just unbearable. Every night, it's as if she were about to die. A passing, but very palpable death. Transitory, but very real. Every night a temporary death.

"It's been going on for months. He hardly sleeps at all."

They fell silent again. Rafael finished his drink and put the glass down on the bedside table. One of the neighbours had the television on. A baseball game. The distant excitement of the commentator was in marked contrast to the dark disorder of their room. Mario Ojeda has just reached second base. The Caracas Lions are in trouble now.

"What if it's us?" asked Silvia in a low voice.

Rafael slid a slow, exploratory hand towards Silvia's body.

"We're fine. Don't worry about it. It could be nothing."

They fell silent again for a few seconds.

"'Nothing' doesn't bleed."

They looked at each other. They moved closer. She stroked his hair. He put his hand on her waist. They fell asleep, their arms about each other.

The following morning, there were three or four more drops of blood on the carpet.

Other People's Correspondence

Take a good man, an apple and a lot of needles.

First: because good people do still exist.

It isn't easy to talk about them. We lack the necessary words or perhaps those words have become so worn with use that they no longer mean anything. When we try to define goodness, it never rings quite true; even the language itself seems suspect. Our vocabulary is corrupt as well. Saying, for example, that someone has noble sentiments, is a naturally kind and loving person who believes in enjoying life to the full and not harming other people, well, it just sounds ridiculous, unbelievable. And yet there are such people. Federico Aranguren is one of them. Kind without being naive, trusting without being ingenuous; caring, unselfish and helpful. He can be mischievous too and has a good sense of humour, so he's no fool. Nor does he flaunt his goodness. Fortunately, he's not religious either. He doesn't seek consolation for his own woes by pointing the finger at others and dishing out the blame. He knows the temptations of this world, but has learned to resist them. It's almost as if he were living a second life, in the same place and in the same body, having already given in to all his weaknesses the first time around. He always makes the right choices and is always happy. He exudes a strange contentment. Sometimes he arouses more surprise than envy.

Aranguren is married. His wife is an administrator, the assistant director of an insurance company. They have a four-year-old daughter, Ximena, whom Aranguren takes to kindergarten every morning, before doing the rounds of the various private schools where he spends his daytime hours. Aranguren teaches literature, art education and world history. After school, he goes to the university, where he's finishing his M.A. He's in his last semester. He wants to write his thesis on literary correspondences. Rather a broad subject, comments his tutor. You should restrict yourself to certain topics, to certain authors. Literary correspondence is almost a genre in itself. It's like wanting to write a thesis on poetry. It's just impossible. Do you understand?

Aranguren does understand, but is not convinced. Optimism is never rational.

On Thursday afternoons, Aranguren doesn't go to the university, but to the prison. He works as a volunteer at the Cárcel del Oeste, a personal initiative he began this year. He went there in person to offer his services, presenting them with a programme of study and assuring them that he simply wanted to help. They accepted his offer. Since then, Aranguren has been teaching a creative writing class, getting prisoners to read and encouraging them to write and put their own experiences into words. The Cárcel del Oeste was intended to hold three thousand prisoners, but it currently houses six thousand. Of those six thousand, eleven chose to join the course. Aranguren is delighted. He likes the number eleven. Literature now has the equivalent of a football team, he says.

It wasn't easy at first. It took him months to gain even a minimal degree of trust. Three of the men were convicted murderers. Three were in for minor robberies, assaults and possession of firearms. One was a born-again Christian and refused to talk about his past. On the cover of his notebook he had written: "Do not steal. God is watching you." The other four were there for various drug-trafficking offences. Half of them were still awaiting sentence. But they all, in one way or another, felt they had been the victims of injustice, the enormous injustice of being alive.

This is the sort of thing that happens to Aranguren during his voluntary work: one afternoon, he arrives a little early and has to wait in the exercise yard. None of his students is there yet, but other prisoners are walking around the yard, sitting down, talking, watching him. Aranguren feels uncomfortable, although he tries to hide it. He avoids looking directly at any of them. Instinct tells him that it's best not to look these people in the eye. He's in a small exercise yard, one of several. There's a guard nearby. Aranguren shouldn't feel nervous, but it's impossible not to in a place like this. You can smell criminality in the air, he thinks. And for a while, he savours these words, touching them with the tip of his tongue, moving them around on his palate. He may even consider it rather original. Inside each of those bodies lurks a kind of disorderly, restless violence, waiting to burst out. Aranguren can sense it. Or at least he thinks he can. Each prisoner is, in a way, a cage. Their bodies provide an order, a grammar, but inside they continue to experience life as something fierce and savage.

A few yards away, a man walks by. He has no shirt on and is talking to himself. He's not mad, he's just talking to himself. His lightweight trousers are held up with a black plastic belt. Suddenly he stops. Without saying a word, he undoes his belt, lowers his trousers and crouches down. He strains and defecates right there, in a corner of the yard. No-one seems to notice. Aranguren observes him out of the corner of one eye, and slowly, carefully, moves closer to the guard. The man stands, pulls up his trousers, buckles his belt and walks off. Then another prisoner moves away from the wall and, from a distance, berates him, shouting: Hey, you! Are you just going to leave that pile of shit for us to look at? He points to the turd in the middle of the courtyard, gleaming in the sunshine.

Second: the red apple.

He bought it off a guy in the street who sells fruit out of crates. There were green and yellow apples too. The green ones were too small, he thought, the yellow ones too expensive. He chose a single apple, the shapeliest, healthiest-looking one.

He and his students have been working together, week after week, for nearly six months. At first, the classes were very didactic. Aranguren would take along an extract from some great classic work. He would read it out loud, comment on it and try to describe the period in which it was written, what the author was trying to do, what stylistic techniques he or she had used and so on. He tried, without much success, to encourage debate, but the prisoners said nothing. They didn't even look at him. On the third Thursday, one of them asked if he could read them something a bit meatier. They were bored. Aranguren began to seek out different texts, to experiment with more modern themes and with writers that his small reading group could relate to. He read Horacio Quiroga, Edgar Allan Poe and John Cheever. He read Salvador Garmendia's story "The Devil Who Couldn't Stand Still" and chapter 7 of Sergei Dovlatov's novel *Ours*. Every Thursday, he tried to surprise them. Then he started setting little exercises. He wanted to get them more involved, to provoke them, to try and get them to participate in some way: "If none of you speaks, then this isn't a workshop," he said.

Last week, they spent over an hour writing a new ending for a story by Oscar Marcano. One night, a man – feared and hated by all the other tenants in an apartment block – leaves his car in someone else's parking space. The following morning, he can't get out: the neighbour whose space he has taken has double-parked her car, blocking him in. Saturday morning. The hated neighbour is pressing the woman's intercom buzzer. Insistently. Furiously. The woman is asleep in bed with her boyfriend. They had only got home in the early hours. The buzzer keeps buzzing. Constantly. Pitilessly. They wake up. She tells her boyfriend about the neighbour, how arrogant and abusive he is and how every-one is shit-scared of him. He doesn't pay the ground rent, flouts all the rules, and shows no respect for anyone. The buzzer keeps grinding away in their ears. Until the boyfriend, torn from sleep, has had enough and decides to take charge of the situation. By this time, there are other people in the car park below. The neighbour has abandoned the intercom buzzer and is now sounding the horn of his car, jumping up and down, screaming and thumping the roof. The boyfriend pushes his way past the onlookers and heads for his girlfriend's car. The neighbour is beside himself with rage. He provokes the other man, confronts him, prods him and, finally, launches a gigantic gob of spit that lands on his forehead. The spit runs down, thick and viscous, as far as his right eye.

Aranguren shut the book.

"What happens next?" he asked.

The prisoners stared at him in bewilderment. He tried to encourage them. It's not that difficult. You can probably all come up with another ending. How would you finish this story? No-one seemed to want to be the first, but eventually each man offered his own conclusion. And in not one of those versions did the abusive neighbour survive. Far better to tell the story of a murder than to commit one. Literature has fewer consequences than life.

This Thursday, Aranguren arrives bearing a red apple. His enthusiasm immediately wanes, however, when he realises that something is wrong. You can smell criminality in the air, he thinks again. And the smell is stronger than ever. The climate has changed. Not all the members of the group are present. Three are missing. No-one offers any explanation, no-one knows anything about the missing men. But it's clear that the situation is far from normal. There are fewer people in the exercise yard. There's something different about the way the prisoners keep looking at each other. They move more quickly. Their gestures are more abrupt. Is something going on? Aranguren asks. No-one answers. Perhaps, he thinks, the only thing that has changed is his own fear. He tries to get a grip on himself. He shows them the apple. I brought this in today, he says. I had an idea for an exercise. Aranguren has decided that the time has come to improvise, to get a little creativity going. He wants to challenge them, to introduce something that has nothing to do with prison. What does an apple mean to them? What's the first thing that comes into their heads? What are they thinking? What are they feeling? Could they perhaps write something about this apple? They sit, looking uncomfortable, in the grip of a tension that, however hard he tries, Aranguren cannot really feel. They are part of it, he is not. You'd better leave, sir, says one of them. He's right, says another. It suddenly occurs to Aranguren that what's happening *does* affect him, that the invisible danger threatens *him* as well. They're right. He should leave. Now.

But that "now" comes too late. Aranguren doesn't even get as far as the metal door that leads out into the passageway. There is an explosion of voices, as if a blaring, cacophonous siren has just been set off. Everything happens so fast that all he can do is throw himself to the floor. His students surround him. He hears shouts, shots, the sound of metal striking metal. A howl, an ever more aggressive chorus of metallic noises. As if the air were made of tin. It even hurts to breathe. As if the sky were full of knives.

The news bulletin on one of the television channels announces that violence has broken out in the prison, an internal battle between rival gangs. Fourteen people have been trapped inside, among them a few special visitors, six lawyers and two volunteer teachers who go there every Thursday. The authorities are trying to bring the situation under control.

Another channel is showing a special report on the over-crowding and violence that is rife in the various penal institutions around the country. Another is showing images from a riot that took place last year in a prison near Ciudad Bolívar, when two gangs came into bloody conflict. There were twenty-seven deaths. The winners ended up playing football with the head of the defeated gang leader.

Aranguren spends several hours trapped in the prison. He's really shaken. He feels like screaming, despairing, panicking, weeping. All he wants is to get out of there. This is no place for human beings, he thinks. He keeps the apple clasped almost obsessively in his hand.

After four hours, the police finally force their way in, using tear gas and firing guns. Aranguren leaves the prison, trembling. The apple still in his hand. Red. Untouched.

That night, he can't sleep. He lies awake until dawn, hoping for more information, for some last-minute bulletin to provide him with a new version of events, a different ending. He's still badly shaken. He peers in at his sleeping daughter, then goes into his study. He sits down and, while he waits, leafs through the bibliography he's been putting together for his thesis. He picks up a book and half-heartedly reads a few pages: the letters William Burroughs wrote to Allen Ginsberg during his journey from Panama to Peru. He alights on this passage: "Every morning a swelling cry goes up from the kids who sell Luckies in the street – 'A *ver* Luckies' 'Look here Luckies' – will they still be saying 'A *ver* Luckies' a hundred years from now? Nightmare fear of stasis. Horror of being finally *stuck* in this place. This fear has followed me all over South America. A horrible sick feeling of final destination."

Aranguren sits thinking about various literary correspondences and finally falls asleep in front of the television.

Third: the needles.

He didn't go back to the prison for three and a half months. His wife made him promise that he wouldn't. Not that he wanted to. Fear is the engine that moves history along. His brief experience of that prison riot had bruised his optimism. His enthusiasm had grown more fragile. In the end, though, it was the prison authorities who phoned and asked him to come back. Even if only for one session. Even if only to close the circle and conclude his educational work. The prisoners themselves had asked him for one last class, they said.

It's Thursday, and Aranguren is sitting with his workshop group. He is nervous and visibly ill at ease. A little embarrassed too. It seems so rude to say goodbye and just get out of there. That's what they would like to do, say goodbye and not come back. Aranguren talks a great deal and very quickly. He tries to summarise what they've done, recalling each text they've read and trying to list some of the things they've learned. He's also brought some books with him as presents. He promises to send more. Maybe he could come back every three months or so. The prisoners listen in silence, exchanging furtive glances. Aranguren begins to feel the same fear he felt before. Like a gust of wind brushing the soles of his feet. There's something wrong. It's happening again. His students reassure him. There are no fights, no riots. They just have a favour to ask. They want him to help them write some letters, letters to the courts, to the public prosecutor, to the newspapers, to the media . . . letters that could help them get out of there. Most of the prisoners are still awaiting trial. Some have even served out their sentences, but are being kept there until the legal bureaucrats get around to giving the orders for their release. The conditions in the prison are totally unacceptable. This place is worse than hell itself. The system's completely fucked, sir. That's all they want him to write. Put more politely, of course. That's all. Can he do it?

Aranguren nods tensely, nervously. Hurriedly. Then he leaves.

A few months later, there's another riot in the same prison. Aranguren watches it live in his apartment, on the television news. He thinks he recognises some of his former students among the prisoners who have overpowered the guards and who are, at that very moment, organising a demonstration on the roof of the main building. The images are truly shocking. Each prisoner is holding a needle. A big needle. Like a spine from a sea urchin. They all hold up their needles, then lift them very slowly to eye level. The needles glitter. Aranguren gets to his feet, unable to take his eyes off the screen. The prisoners then stick the needles into their lips and begin stitching. Stick the needle in. Push. Pull. Now the other lip. Stick the needle in. Push. Pull.

They are bleeding.

In front of the cameras, the prisoners are sewing their lips together. Aranguren suddenly remembers the workshop. When he can stand the images no longer, he turns off the television. He picks up a book. But he can't bear to behave as if nothing were happening. He is suddenly filled with a horrible sick feeling of final destination. He turns on the television again. The prisoners, their lips full of needles, are sitting on the roof of the prison. Waiting.

Time is the only perfect crime.

A Mexican Story

My friend Lencho Mejía has been murdered thirty-seven times in Los Angeles, five in Tijuana and once in a Romanian-Argentinian co-production filmed in Honduras, which came very close to being nominated for an Oscar as Best Foreign Language Film. Only twice, though, has he had the chance to say anything before dropping dead: "You fucking bastard!" on both occasions. He had to say it quickly and quietly, but he put a lot of feeling into it. Everything he learned from Stanislavski is encapsulated in those three words. Or so Lencho always says when, at home, after his fifth tequila, he gets out his videos and makes us watch all his deaths, one after another.

My relationship with Hilda began on just such a night. I'd also had several tequilas and was perched on the arm of a small sofa. She was beside me. Lencho was sitting next to her, poised, rather like an insect, leaning towards the television screen. Hilda brushed my left knee with her hand.

"It was the lousy editor who fucked me up here. I don't know why he didn't use the other take, where you could see me from the front and where the fall was more dramatic. I even spat on the ground. It was my best angle too."

Hilda again ran her hand over my knee. There was no way this could have been an accident. When you're that close to someone, accidents don't happen. I looked at her out of the corner of my eye, but she seemed completely absent, absorbed, staring at the screen, almost as if she'd never seen those images before. Her fingers, however, kept hovering close to my leg, as if quite innocently. I tried to appear natural and changed position slightly, but left my leg where it was, in contact with her hand. Then, suddenly, she started gently scratching my leg with one of her nails, at least I think she did.

"This is the bit I'm always telling you about, Javier. Concentrate now, so that you don't miss the hand. It appears on the right side of the screen. It's only there for a second, but it's Antonio Banderas's hand. Really. Look!"

Hilda pinched me. I felt the warmth of her fingers squeezing my leg, calling to me from the other side of my trousers. Why was she doing that? Why was she touching me like that while, on the screen, her husband was dying over and over?

Lencho and I have been friends for a long time. We met through another actor, soon after I arrived in Mexico. An immediate empathy sprang up between us, a natural trust, as if we were childhood friends who had unexpectedly found each other again. Lencho got me my first job as a lighting assistant. I had almost no experience, but he was incredibly supportive and always on hand with really good advice. He also acted as guarantor when I rented the apartment in Colonia Nápoles, which is also where he took refuge when he split up with Mónica. We lived together for a few months while he sorted himself out. A few months before that, he had started working for Channel 7, where he met Hilda and fell madly in love. Hilda was fourteen years younger than him, but they were really good together. Hilda was stunningly beautiful. They got married in August, two years ago now. I was a witness at the ceremony.

From that evening on, I began to feel uncomfortable. I kept thinking about Lencho, about our friendship, but I was troubled, too, by the thought of Hilda. Her image would surface in my mind out of nowhere, as if it were lying in wait for me somewhere deep inside. I couldn't help it. I couldn't control my imagination either. She kept reappearing. Naked, lying face down on some blue sheets, lifting her hips slightly, her buttocks. Even in the dark, her skin glowed. Or I would imagine her bent over my cock, working it with her lips, licking it with her tongue. At other times, I would see only her eyes, like liquid coal, coming towards me, fixed on mine, until she was near enough to touch me. Even before I started masturbating while thinking about her, I already felt dirty, because of Lencho. Which is stronger, friendship or desire?

I stopped going to their apartment altogether and tried to meet up with him in places where I was sure he'd be alone. And whenever he invited me back to his place, I'd come up with some excuse, some reason not to go, however ridiculous, silly or childish. I was doing this for his sake, I was protecting him. I didn't trust myself. And I was quite right not to. I knew that if I saw Hilda, I would succumb immediately to the slightest temptation,

I wouldn't be able to control myself. I often used to imagine her making coffee in her kitchen. She's wearing a green dress that drapes perfectly over her hips. Lencho is in the bathroom or has gone to the bedroom looking for some video or other. Hilda hasn't yet seen me. Her shoulders are bare. Her hair falls in a loose tangle on the back of her neck. I am one step away from biting her. The danger is growing all the time. I've already had too many solitary orgasms, I already had a whole private collection of sighs and sobs stored up just for her, waiting for her.

When I saw her at Fat Hernández's house, my balls felt as though they'd filled up with ice cubes. I felt dizzy and sick. She was happy and smiling, talking to Maite Iturria and Aleida Ponce. Her eyes met mine, but that was all. She didn't even say hello. It was at a party to celebrate finishing work on a documentary about the Huichol people. It had turned out really well, and everyone was in celebratory mood. They were mainly people from Channel 11, and it hadn't even occurred to me that Lencho and his wife would be there. I hardly drank anything all night, feeling restless and awkward. I didn't speak to Hilda once, but I could sense all the time that she was there, that even when I couldn't see her, she was sending out meaningful looks, secret, insinuating signals aimed only at me. I was also doing my best to avoid Lencho. When the situation became unbearable, I decided to leave early, but as I was leaving, I met her by the bathroom door. I stopped and immediately lowered my eyes, as if I were guilty as charged.

"Anyone would think you were afraid of me," she said.

I raised my eyes and looked at her. At that moment, a plump girl emerged from the bathroom, leaving the door open. The walls were covered in green ceramic tiles. Green like the dress I imagine you wearing. Like when you're making coffee in the kitchen. Like when your hair falls in a tangle on the back of your neck. Like when I bite you.

"Fancy joining me in the bathroom?" she said with an ambiguous smile that still left room for doubt: Is she serious? Is this a joke?

When I got home, I masturbated again. Everything was green.

Lencho went off for four days' filming in Sinaloa. It was a big project, a film starring Cate Blanchett. Two days later, Hilda called and asked me to go and see her. She needed to talk to me. I spent whole hours trembling and indecisive. The two of us would be alone together. My mouth filled with saliva at the mere possibility. Lencho should never have accepted that job. Lencho shouldn't have gone so far away. Lencho shouldn't have left his wife on her own. I kept repeating these things to myself. Ever more vehemently. Lencho shouldn't have done this to me; you don't do that kind of thing to a friend.

I decided not to go, then five minutes later decided I would. I spent several hours going to and fro like that. There was a ping-pong table inside my head, and I was in the middle, bouncing back and forth, getting more and more nervous. As eight o'clock approached, my excitement intensified. As usual, I made the very worst decision: I decided to go and see Hilda, but only in order to tell her no. To make it clear to her, in a gesture of male solidarity, that Lencho and I were best mates, that she and I should abandon this absurd little game once and for all, and that I would never betray a brother.

As soon as I entered the apartment, I began to kiss her, touch her and remove her clothes. We made love right there, in the living room, on the sofa, in front of the television. The opaque screen dimly reflected our gestures, our desperately clinging bodies, one on top of the other, one inside the other. We touched each other clumsily, urgently, frantically. It was all a single, seamless journey from the front door being opened to the last yelp of pleasure, the two of us naked by then and lying on the cold floor tiles. The second time we made love more calmly. We explored each other's skin, caressed each other, licked each other. There were more kisses than bites. At half past eleven Lencho phoned. Hilda allowed the phone to ring several times, until the answering machine came on. We listened to his message in silence. I poured myself a tequila.

I went two weeks without seeing either of them. Lencho tried to get in touch a couple of times, but I always managed to avoid him. Hilda sent me a few emails. I didn't answer those either. On the afternoon that Hilda called me on my mobile, I was just on the point of taking a job in Guadalajara. She sounded really frightened. She didn't so much speak as push the words out into the air.

"I think he suspects something," she said. "I think Lencho has found us out."

That was all she said, then she abruptly hung up. Ten minutes later, my phone rang again. I thought it must be her phoning back. I felt really jittery. My hands were cold. It was Lencho. He was calling me from a film producer's office. He was his usual natural, friendly self. Affectionate and very calm. I found myself thinking that perhaps Hilda's phone call had been a bad dream, a product of all the fears and guilt inside my head. Lencho said he had something very important to tell me. We need to have a serious talk, he said. He made me promise to go to his apartment that evening, just to chat, like in the good old days, that's what he said, and have a few drinks, he added, because we never seem to see each other anymore, Javier. We need to have a serious talk, he said again. After all, you're my best mate, he said, my brother.

Should I go? And why? It certainly was a very strange situation. I tried several times to call Hilda, but without success. If Lencho really had found out about us, why was he being so nice to me, why was he inviting me to his apartment? Was it purely out of friendship, or was this part of some terrible, twisted plot, a plan to have his revenge on us both? Where was Hilda? What had happened to her? Perhaps he was keeping her a prisoner in her own home. Perhaps he had hurt her. Which is stronger, friendship or desire?

He embraced me warmly, as he always did. He poured us each a large tequila and started telling me about the filming in Sinaloa. He was alone, or so it seemed. Of course, Hilda might have been in the bedroom, or in the bathroom, or perhaps at a friend's house. Or perhaps dead. I didn't dare to ask about her.

"That Cate Blanchett is seriously cool."

But I couldn't stop thinking about Hilda. I was looking at Lencho sitting there on the sofa, and remembering Hilda's tremulous voice on the phone. Then, on the blank television screen, as if I were watching a recording, I began to see images of Hilda and me making love on that sofa. Hilda and me naked, desperately biting and licking and touching each other. Right in the spot where Lencho was now sitting, drinking tequila, talking to me and smiling.

"Have you heard that story about Güero Palma?" Lencho's voice distracted me from the screen.

"No," I said.

"Because ever since I've been back, I've kept thinking about it. Güero Palma was from Sinaloa," he said. "He was a drug dealer, but an unusual kind of guy. He had a great friend, a Venezuelan called Flores or something. They were real mates. But the Venezuelan betrayed him. He stole his wife from him. She fell for him and off they went. They became lovers and headed north. And since the wife was one of the signatories on Güero's bank accounts, they got a lot of money out of him. Something like two million dollars."

Lencho picked up the bottle and poured himself another drink. I covered my glass with my hand.

"What? You're not drinking?"

"Later."

Lencho nodded and put the bottle down on the table again.

"But the Venezuelan was a complete arsehole. After taking the money, he killed Güero's wife. And he didn't stop there. He put the wife's head in a metal box, filled it with dry ice, then sent it back to Güero in Mexico. Here's a nice little present for you, you lousy bastard."

Lencho smiled.

"And people say we Mexicans are violent," he added.

He looked at me as if expecting some comment, some reaction to what he had just told me. I said nothing. I couldn't speak. We sat for a while in silence. Lencho didn't take his eyes off me. Nor did he stop smiling. I nodded, as if I were pondering what to say. When I could stand the silence no longer, I stood up and said I had to go to the toilet.

I couldn't pee either. My penis was a tiny creature in retreat, trying to escape inside my body. I couldn't squeeze out a single drop. I washed my face, looked at myself in the mirror, as if searching for some sign. All I could see was a slender line of sweat next to my left ear. I felt cold, but I was sweating too. But only there, just next to my left ear. I decided that there was nothing for it, I had to take a chance. I crept out of the bathroom, leaving the door slightly ajar. I tried to tread as lightly as I could, so as not to make any noise. I knew every inch of the apartment. I'd helped them move in. I walked to the end of the corridor, as far as the main bedroom. The door was closed. I rapped gently, each rap slightly faster than the last. I whispered her name. Hilda. Again I glanced down at the end of the corridor, towards the living room. Hilda. I placed my hand on the door handle. I opened the door. I heard Lencho clear his throat or cough. There was no-one in the room. The bed was unmade. All I saw was a red sock lying next to one of the pillows. In the living room something creaked. Lencho getting up from the sofa, I thought. I closed the bedroom door. I hurried back to the bathroom. I went in. I heard a whistle. I left the door half-open while I flushed the toilet.

On my way back, I stopped in the kitchen. I poured myself a glass of water and glanced hurriedly around, still looking for some clue, looking for who knows what. Next to a wooden chopping board I saw a large sharp knife, two potatoes and half a red onion. Lencho asked me something. I heard his voice, but didn't understand what he was saying. I was feeling worse and worse. Lencho again asked a question. It sounded like an incomprehensible, formless croak.

"It's O.K., I'm just getting a glass of water. I'll be right there."

When I went back into the room, Lencho was already standing up, putting on a leather jacket.

"You took your time," he muttered, still smiling.

I merely nodded and avoided his eyes.

"Right then," he said. "Are you coming?"

"Where?" I asked, trying to sound as casual as possible.

"To fetch Hilda. She's at her mother's house." He paused, scowled slightly, but continued smiling. "Don't you want to see her?"

*

How could I refuse? We walked slowly to the front door, but before opening it, he paused for a moment and turned to face me. He remained like that for a few seconds, as if deciding what to do, what to say. A dark shadow scurried past behind his eyes. Still looking at me, he opened his mouth, but no sound came out. He spoke to me in silence, letting me read his lips. Just three words, spoken very slowly. Just three words. The three words he said on those two occasions when he had a speaking part – just before he fell to the ground, dead.

Stray Bullets

FOR IBSEN MARTÍNEZ

No-one heard the shots.

It was impossible to hear anything above the racket made by the demonstration: the noise of people talking, shouting, chanting slogans or blowing whistles. And then there was the music. Not to mention some of the demonstration leaders, who, from their different vantage points, were haranguing the demonstrators through loudhailers. It was 3.00 in the afternoon. Their words bounced about in the sunlight. The bullets went unnoticed. And it was only when bodies started falling that anyone realised the bullets had arrived, that they were there.

The first to fall was a girl. Yolimar Martínez. Nineteen, an undergraduate and a member of the Simón Rodríguez Student Brigade. She joined the demonstration to support the government. All she remembers is feeling a sudden burning sensation in her back, not the normal heat you feel on a hot day, but as if she were being scalded. It all happened very quickly. She felt herself falling backwards, and there was nothing she could grab hold of; she just lost her balance and couldn't understand why, as if gravity had suddenly become a ferocious force, as if the earth were swallowing her up. A cloud flashed past her eyes and

49

vanished. The same thing happened with the tops of the trees, a streetlamp, the surprised eyes of two friends, the knees of some other bodies, until her head thudded onto the tarmac.

A couple of yards further on, almost at the same moment, Idelmaro Jiménez fell too. At sixty-five, he's in good physical shape, and obviously takes regular exercise. He's part of the Andrés Bello Teachers' Committee, one of the organisations behind the protest march. He felt something bite into his shoulder. As if a fishing hook had dropped down from the skies and caught him. Instinctively, he raised his hand to his collar bone, but before he could touch it, he collapsed. He couldn't stop himself. He saw the tarmac rising up to meet him.

In a matter of seconds, there was a huge stir. Blood is a very effective explosive, even more so than gunpowder. It's a substance so private that it never fails to provoke panic when even one drop of the stuff appears in public. In a matter of seconds, there were screams, people running and stumbling. No-one knew quite how to react. A few crouched down to help the wounded. The police and the soldiers responded with violence: they did their job. They did what they were trained to do. They barged their way through the crowd, shouting and hitting and shoving. One officer even fired into the air, apparently aiming at the clouds. But Latin America bears very little resemblance to what you see in films, even in films made here. The shot only provoked more hysteria, more stampedes.

Six hours later, the city governor was on all the national tele-vision channels reporting that a total of twelve people had been slightly injured and four seriously, one of whom was in the intensive care unit at the military hospital. The government and the opposition exchanged accusations. "Normality has been restored," said the governor.

"Oh, dear God, it's Henry!"

The old man stood up at the table and desperately started fumbling around for the remote control. The others looked at him, not really understanding what was going on. The old man stopped and pointed at the screen. They all turned to follow his finger.

"I've just seen Henry!" he shouted.

The news, however, had moved on, and all they were showing now was, yet again, the city governor reluctantly answering the journalists' questions. The old man took a while to calm down. He drank two glasses of water. With him were his wife Carmen and his two other children, Omar and Fanny. He finally managed to explain what he had seen. He assured them that among the images of the demonstration in the city centre, he had spotted his oldest child, Henry. As clear as day. It was him. In the middle of all that chaos. Someone had shot him. He saw him fall to the ground. Wounded. Why don't you believe me, dammit, it was Henry.

The supper instantly cooled. The plates of food lay shipwrecked on the pale green tablecloth. Carmen began to cry nervously, fearing the worst. Omar, the youngest of the siblings, kept switching channels, trying to catch the images on some other news programme, while Fanny was on the phone, trying to locate Henry. To no avail. No-one had heard from him. His wife, Virginia, was already home, wondering why Henry hadn't yet arrived and hadn't even called: Is he with you? Has something happened? Fanny, tell me!

They brought in two smaller television sets from the bedrooms. They placed the three sets side by side on the dining-room table and tuned each one to a different channel. Fanny again called Virginia and asked her to monitor the state channel, just in case they re-broadcast the same images. They sat down in front of the three screens and waited.

"Isn't there anything else we can do?" asked Carmen, her voice still choked with tears.

Her husband brusquely told her to be quiet, his eyes glued to the screens. Growing increasingly anxious, Carmen burst out:

"Can't we call someone? Can't we go and look for him? Is watching television the only thing we can do?"

"Shhh!"

At 9.18 that night, in a brief news round-up in the middle of the current soap opera, they all saw the sequence that had so troubled Henry's father. They all leaned forward, holding their breath. Carmen and Fanny stood up. It really was Henry. They all saw him. The camera showed him looking anxious and bewildered, as if he had become caught up in that story by accident, by chance, as the result of some confusion. Suddenly, Henry collapsed in on himself.

"Oh, my God!" cried Carmen, crying and clinging to her husband's arm. The others stood there frozen, eyes fixed on the screen.

It only lasted a moment. Then Henry disappeared. As if someone had cut off his legs. As if he had simply emptied out. Henry crumpled to the ground.

Then the camera shifted to a group of women who were screaming and trying to get away from the crowd. More shots were heard. Moving erratically around, the camera seemed to be trying to pursue these shots, trying vainly to track them down. Finally, the filming stopped and a grave-faced presenter announced that there would be more footage, much more, at eleven o'clock, on the main news. See you there.

The phone rang and they all rushed to answer it. The receiver almost flew through the air until Omar managed to catch it and say hello.

"Hello?" he said again tentatively, surrounded by the watchful eyes of his family.

All he could hear was his sister-in-law crying. He held the receiver up, as if it were a tiny loudspeaker, so that everyone could hear. In the background. A remote croaking. A series of damp interjections. A hiccup at the far end of a tunnel.

When they turned off the three televisions, they sat there wrapped in an electric silence. The air around them bristled. Now all they could hear was Carmen's breathing, interspersed by faint moans. The small apartment, in the south-west of the city, had become a precipice. A precipice on the fourteenth floor.

"Now what do we do? What are we going to do?"

They tried to organise themselves and share out the various tasks. The main thing was not to allow themselves to be overwhelmed by distress. Or by pessimism. Everyone knows that bad news travels fast, so there was still hope that he was alive. However, any hopes had soon foundered on the images of Henry disappearing into himself, melting away in the middle of that crowd. There they were, repeated over and over. As if behind the eyes of each of them a new television channel was being premiered, a secret, almost private channel, devoted exclusively to broadcasting those same images, again and again, without pause. Henry Lucena was now that private channel, that endless wound.

Virginia came round so that she and Carmen could keep each other company. They would stay there, watching and waiting, hoping to be surprised by a phone call or by the arrival of Henry himself, safe and sound, with the best of anecdotes to tell. The father went to the morgue, Omar to the military hospital, and it fell to Fanny to go to the television channel to ask for a copy of the footage shown on the news.

She was the only one to have any success.

There was a queue at the morgue. The father was given a paper ticket bearing the handwritten number "19". The atmosphere was positively hostile. He had to stand, trying to keep calm. Beside him, a young girl, dressed for a party, was crying non-stop. Her make-up had left a dark, unpleasant stain on her face. Her clothes were all rumpled. The father glanced at her legs. They were beautiful, he thought, then immediately felt ashamed. A fly drifted past. By the time they called his number, an hour and a half had passed. The girl behind him was still crying.

There were six as yet unclaimed corpses, unidentified by any family member. The father leaned over each body, feeling colder and colder. A dank, sticky cold that seeped into his skin and stained his clothes. His throat was frozen, his fingers stiff. With long experience apparent in every gesture, a male nurse slid back the sheet covering each body, meanwhile looking the father fixedly in the eye, trying to anticipate the impact of the moment of recognition, if there was one. Some bodies smelled worse than others. The old man struggled to control his feelings of nausea and fear. When he saw the last body, when he saw that his son was not there in that cellar, he almost burst into tears. The nurse lit a cigarette. "You can come back later, if you like," he said.

There was no sign of Henry Lucena at the military hospital either. Omar made such a fuss that they allowed him to take a look at the badly wounded patient who had been brought in after the demonstration. He was a chubby-cheeked lad, who still bore the shock of what had happened imprinted on his face. He had regained consciousness, but was still under observation in intensive care. An officer on duty advised Omar to go to the other hospitals in the city, which he did. He went to the A. & E. departments of another three, but with the same result – nothing. He was the last to return to the apartment, by which time it was 2.00

in the morning. They were all exhausted, their eyes puffy, a look of unease on their faces. On the larger of the televisions they were watching the images Fanny had managed to acquire: Henry, silent, with the sound off. The father kept pressing the remote control, mechanically repeating the sequence over and over. They were high on caffeine. They all felt so powerless. Where could he be? Why had he just disappeared like that? There must be a reason, some potent reason why he didn't phone or just turn up. Something really bad must have happened to him. Why didn't he get in touch? Why, at this late hour, did they still not know where he was? Henry was only present on the television screen. That was the only place where they could see him moving, always the same pre-recorded movements. Only there was he alive.

The argument began at dawn. None of them had been able to sleep. Their eyes were dry, their mouths gritty, their skin rough. It was just unbearable being there, unable to do anything, waiting for it to be 8.00 in the morning and for the country to get back to work. When she put another pot of coffee in the middle of the table, Carmen also gave vent to her despair and muttered some anti-government sentiment. Omar reacted at once, answering back, contradicting her: the president had nothing to do with what had happened. Their words collided in mid-air. A sound of clashing metal wrapped around them all. The father stood up too. Fanny, who was lying on the sofa, began talking out loud, without looking at anyone, as if she were intoning a lament. They all talked at the same time, gabbling, letting off steam. This was nothing new in the family. They had been divided and at odds for a long time, especially Carmen and Omar. In fact, one year, mother and son, dreading the political flimflam and vulgar sentimentality of New Year's Eve television, had promised not to talk about politics anymore, not to allow politics to drive a wedge between them. Omar actively supported the government. He was a member of the Bolívar Committee at work. He was a regular at national demonstrations and, on four occasions, had been government representative at a polling station. His mother couldn't stand the president. She thought him coarse and aggressive. She couldn't bear his melodramatic style. She didn't believe in him. Father and daughter took a more considered view. They found both extremes irritating and found it equally irritating to be constantly arguing about them. They were sick to death of the whole thing. And yet, on this occasion, all four had something to say. Only a shout from Virginia managed to stop them:

"Please, that's enough! Shut up!"

She was beside herself, almost hysterical. She had her hair drawn back in an elastic band. Her red-lidded eyes looked very small. Her lips were puffy too, as if all her anxious chewing on them had made them grow drastically in size. In the face of her anguish and grief, the others felt intimidated, perhaps even a little ridiculous. She was Henry's wife. She hadn't always been part of the family. Virginia and Henry had married the previous year, ten months ago. For her, he wasn't the past, he was the future. He wasn't just blood, but pure love, as random and fortuitous as it was intense and definitive.

"You lot don't understand a thing, do you?" she went on, angry and hurt, her voice broken by sobs. "Don't you know Henry at all? He hated all this. It almost got to the point where he didn't want to come here anymore. Henry doesn't give a toss about politics. He doesn't give a toss about the government or the opposition or any of that stuff! Instead of bickering among yourselves, why don't you think about that?" She stepped forward and pointed at the three televisions. "It's just incredible, don't you think? Just crazy. He hated all this. He would never in his life have gone on a march. Whenever he saw a demonstration, he'd head off in the opposite direction. So why? What was Henry doing there?"

No-one spoke. It was true. Henry himself used to say, with a certain cheeky cynicism, that he was militantly apathetic.

"So what was he doing in the middle of that crowd, eh?" Virginia waved her hands about, as if she were mixing up all her questions in the air. "Don't you find that odd? What was Henry doing there?"

No-one dared to suggest that perhaps he had just happened to be passing and . . . No, that wasn't even a possibility. Virginia was right. Her husband and politics didn't even have a *passing* acquaintance. He felt an almost physical, chemical repugnance for all the overheated public debate gripping society. "Political contamination," he called it. He thought the country was sick.

At precisely 6.00 in the morning, with disconcerting exactitude, the phone rang. The father answered. A neutral voice asked to speak to Fanny. It was the television channel wanting to follow up the case, asking if they could send round a reporter to do an interview. Fanny covered the receiver with one hand.

"What shall I say?"

Omar refused point-blank to have anything to do with it. It was obvious to him that the channel was pro-opposition. They just wanted to manipulate the facts. They wanted to take advantage of the situation to attack the government.

"Forget about politics for once," said his mother. "Think of your brother. It's a good opportunity to get some publicity, to bring him back."

They had a brief discussion. Neither the father nor Fanny trusted the television people's intentions or the use they might make of Henry's disappearance.

"Look, the government only cares about things that appear on T.V.," argued Carmen. As far as she was concerned, anything was worth trying if it would help find her son.

Virginia was in two minds. She didn't want television poking its nose into her private life. She knew that once that particular sluice gate was open, it would be very hard to stop or even control the ensuing rush of journalistic greed. Letting them in meant agreeing to being invaded, to allowing other people – everyone – to snoop on her life, her apartment, the empty space in the bed where her husband should be. That was what made news, that empty space, one that had to be filled with information, but also with melodrama, with sentimentality. They would all, in some way, have to be participants in that absence. They knew this.

Television is pretty straightforward really, a kind of fast-food approach to knowledge. No-one would willingly expose themselves like that, but the urgency of the situation didn't allow for such subtleties. In this instance, the television screen seemed to be their only way out. They said yes. Omar got angry and left the apartment in a huff. He didn't say anything, but there was definitely something threatening about his gestures. Needless to say, he slammed the door behind him.

On the midday news, the commercial channel broadcast a special report from the apartment of the Lucena family, who have been living in a state of high anxiety since last night, when Henry, a family member, disappeared. Our cameras have come here in order to show our viewers what is actually going on in this country. With us are Doña Carmen, Henry's mother, who, as you can see, is very upset, indeed she told us that none of them slept at all last night. Tell us what's been happening, Señora. Tell us what's happening with your son?

Carmen could barely speak. Her words quickly became tears and saliva. We don't know anything about my son. He may be dead. We haven't been told anything. Not by the hospital, the police or anyone. He may have been killed.

They arrived at 8.00 in the morning with a mobile unit, two cameras, a lighting technician with some light screens, a sound engineer, a director and two assistants. The female reporter turned up half an hour later. Everyone in the neighbourhood came out to watch and comment. The last time a television crew had been there was when an alleged drug trafficker had been bumped off in Block 2. That was six months ago. They came, filmed the chalk outline on the ground and left.

The father didn't want to talk. Fanny remained aloof and obviously preferred not to get too involved. She answered only one question, lowering her head and almost mumbling. The sound engineer holding the cordless microphone gave her a knowing wink. Virginia was the one who talked most. Vehemently but not hysterically. She understood the dynamic. She had learned it from day after day of watching news programmes. Immediately after the first question, she stopped looking at the reporter and looked directly into the camera. As if the authorities or those who had the power to resolve the problem were watching and listening to her, talking to her. We just want Henry back.

"They just want Henry back," says the reporter at the end, in a shot taken out in the street. She is standing in the foreground, silhouetted against the tall buildings in the south-west of the city. She is still surrounded by curious onlookers. They are waiting for some response from the authorities. A government that is always talking about human rights should act swiftly and efficiently and clear up this case as quickly as possible. What happened? Where *is* Henry Lucena?

The father turned off the television and gave his wife a somewhat melancholy look. Fanny wasn't overly enthusiastic either.

"Just wait and see," said Virginia, hoping to get her mother-in-law's support. "It will work. Now they'll have to get their act together."

At which point, the phone rang. Virginia smiled, feeling that fate was proving her right. The father made a gesture, indicating that she should answer.

"I bet it'll be more journalists," he murmured.

Virginia didn't even have time to say hello. As soon as she put the phone to her ear, she heard what she heard and immediately repeated it:

"Switch to Channel 8!"

The father again turned the television on.

Omar was being interviewed live in one of the studios owned by the state-run channels. The interviewer, with studied irony, was showing him images from the programme just broadcast on the commercial channel, inviting him to comment on what he was seeing and to give them an alternative interpretation of events. You can see how the channel is manipulating people. There's your mum, right? Well, it's obvious that she's nervous and worried, as she would be, but then watch what the reporter does. She uses your mother's pain and anxiety to ask insidious, leading questions. Rewind it, will you? I want you to see what happened with the first or second question she asked, I don't know if you noticed, Omar. There, do you see?

"*Hijo de puta!*" muttered Virginia. "The bastard!" The words emerged directly from her oesophagus and arrived in her mouth still warm and moist.

The four of them were watching themselves on a screen within a screen. The father moved nearer. He sat down on a stool very close to the television. Omar seemed perfectly natural and at ease.

62

No-one could recall him ever having been on television before, and yet he spoke so clearly and confidently, with such authority. It was all very paradoxical. Now, Omar and the presenter were looking at *them*, observing *them* talking in the apartment. They would pause the images, discuss each one and point at them. When Virginia appeared, the presenter froze the image.

"Who is this?"

"My sister-in-law."

"The wife of your brother, the one who's disappeared."

"Exactly."

"Now, look, I don't know her or anything about her, and I don't want to judge her, but I can tell you that if I was in your situation, if something similar were to happen to my wife or my partner, I wouldn't go running to the media, I wouldn't be making a big performance out of all this. I would first exhaust all the official, legal resources. That's what this country's institutions are there for . . ."

"That's precisely what I told her."

"The bastard!" The words, tense and acidic, were hissed out again from between palate and tongue.

The father turned and gave Virginia a bemused look. The light from the screen glowed faintly on her right cheek.

"Isn't he just doing what we did this morning?" he asked.

Virginia, jaw clenched, was still observing her brother-in-law's image on the screen. Omar thinks that his brother will turn up soon, that he must be in some other hospital or police station, that they should just wait for the authorities to do their job.

"Regrettably, your sister-in-law has been drawn into this whole perverse media game," said the presenter. "Not that we're doubting her good faith, of course, but we really cannot defend such overt manipulation, whose sole aim is to frighten people. It's all part of the opposition's plan to overthrow the government. I wouldn't be surprised if they started claiming that your brother was an opposition leader, if they tried to turn him into a hero, a martyr. They're quite capable of that. They're quite capable of saying that the government killed Henry Lucena."

Virginia's mobile phone rang twice. Instead of a normal ringtone, it played a few seconds from the chorus of one of Julieta Venegas's biggest hits: *The present moment is all we have, the present is all there is.*

"Hello," Virginia said cautiously.

"Is that Virginia Fernández?"

"Yes, speaking."

"Hi. This is Alicia Batista from the TV news. Could you possibly be here at six to be interviewed on our main news programme?"

That same night, the disappearance of Henry Lucena began to take on the status of a national enigma. Who was he? Where was he? What had happened to him? The images from the demonstration were repeated again and again. These were pored over by various analysts on different channels, who speculated as to whether or not he actually had been wounded and, if so, what kind of bullet had been used and where had it come from. A lot of witnesses came forward too. A forthright lady with beady eyes said on one programme that she had exchanged a few words with Henry shortly before "the massacre".

"He's a decent man. Very calm. He was on our side. I heard him shouting anti-government slogans."

On another channel, a tall young man, with very long arms, claimed to have known Henry. They weren't friends exactly, but acquaintances. They worked in the same part of town and sometimes went to the same café. They were together at the demonstration and separated just before "the attack".

"He told me himself that he was fed up with these opposition wimps, fed up with all these demonstrations, with the disorder in the streets. Henry is a natural Bolivarian. That's why he was there."

Soon, there were too many witnesses. And all, it seemed, were perfectly sincere. They spoke with great frankness. They didn't appear to be putting on an act or following a script. It was very hard to know who, on either side of the argument, was pretending. Listening to them, you immediately felt that they were utterly genuine, that what they were saying was true. One night, at the spot where it happened, a mass was held in solidarity with the Lucena family. The following night, in the same spot, a vigil was held, again in solidarity with the Lucena family. On both occasions, there were calls for justice and prayers for peace. One night, Omar was the main protagonist; the next night, Virginia was the centre of attention. Carmen appeared alongside them on both occasions, clasping a handkerchief. She lived divided between the two of them, but sustained by the same anxiety. Each time one of them said or did something, the other would immediately respond by saying or doing something else. Meanwhile, the authorities had failed to solve the case or find an answer. Time was passing, and the trail was growing cold. It was as if, that afternoon, Henry Lucena had simply evaporated. Every line of investigation by the police ended up in the same place: nowhere. The country was ever more attentive, ever more avid for news. Henry Lucena was a national confusion. A well-managed mystery. Every day, whether through television, radio or the rumour mill, people continued to follow the case very closely. There was always something new. One Thursday, Henry's supposed diary unexpectedly turned up. A blue notebook with lined pages, in which daily facts rubbed shoulders with rather cryptic jottings that could be interpreted in various ways. "13 February. Buy chicken. How long are we going to go on like this?" "25 June. Phone Fanny / The lizard's birthday." And further down the page, after a few lines that had been crossed out in black ink: "Get away. Like hell." But the sentence that provoked most head-scratching was the one written in the middle of the entry for 8 August: "I heard her today and felt disgusted." For several days, various programmes spent time analysing and interpreting this supposed confession in this supposed diary. A group of university students scoured newspaper archives, trying to link those words to some public statement issued that day in the national media. A graphologist appeared on a late-night television show, commenting at length on Henry Lucena's scribble.

Every week, the Minister for Citizens' Security promised new results, calling on people not to use the case to gain any political advantage, and every week, more news appeared that spread still more confusion. A journalist in the south of the country discovered a mass grave in a park planted with palm trees. He suggested that one of the skeletons might belong to Henry Lucena. In Caracas, the police raided a cooperative that produced T-shirts bearing Lucena's face on the front. On the back, next to a raised clenched fist, the red shirts declared: "We want justice!" The blue shirts showed Lucena's face accompanied by just one word: "Disappeared!" Printed on the back was a familiar opposition slogan: "Onwards!" The small business also produced posters and placards for both sides. A few days before, a television clairvoyant had predicted that the police were about to unearth an important fact. However, she herself, in a nasal voice and with a grim glint in her eyes, said that there were still many as yet unresolved mysteries. "Henry is neither alive nor dead," she declared. She was accused of being a fraud, and various other psychics and experts in supernatural communications began to surface. They all came up with some new version of Lucena's invisible presence. The authorities finally decided to intervene when a well-known theatrical producer hired the baseball stadium for a spectacle advertised as "The Battle of the Mediums". The publicity suggested that, at the end of the show, on the stage itself, among all the smoke and strange vibrations, a miracle might occur. Faith moves mountains. Be there!

*

Omar and Virginia hadn't seen each other since that first night, since Henry disappeared. He did not return to his parents' apartment on the fourteenth floor. And she moved out of the place she had shared with Henry. She had to flee the plague of phone calls. She couldn't open the front door without finding a journalist wanting to ask her a question or a photographer wanting to take her picture. Her existence had become one long news item. Something similar was happening to Omar. Gradually, though, they were both becoming used to this new dynamic, to this new life. Gradually, they were finding it less unsettling and were even beginning to enjoy the change. Omar has been nominated by the official party as a candidate for mayor of his local council. Virginia now fronts an early-morning radio programme, which began life as a diary of her experiences, but has ended up being a shared space where ordinary people can call in and vent their feelings. It's a kind of virtual complaints department. Therapy at the turn of the dial. "The Worms' Turn" is its title.

Publicly, though, they're still at daggers drawn. Although they haven't met face to face, they have traded insults and mutual accusations at their respective public events. Virginia accuses her brother-in-law of trying to make Henry into an official hero, who gave his life in defence of the government, a martyr executed by anti-government snipers. Omar accuses Virginia of manipulating his brother's image and of allowing him to be used by political interests whose sole aim is to destabilise the country. The father, Carmen and Fanny have been sidelined. Rendered silent. They barely exist.

Two months ago, an ex-boyfriend of Fanny had wangled them the appointment. The three of them went to see him. Superintendent Rincón had been in charge of various state security units and was currently working as advisor to the new national police. He was a gaunt-faced man of few words. They never once saw him light a cigarette, and yet the fingers of his right hand were completely yellow. He received them in the third-floor office of a small building that bore no official identification.

"I don't have much time," he said, by way of greeting.

The three nodded gratefully. The father and mother sat down, and Fanny remained standing.

"You know why we're here."

He did indeed know, but he had no answers to give them. Henry Lucena was one of a tiny percentage of unsolved cases, he said. They had done everything they could to find him, to close the case, but without success. He wanted to be absolutely frank with them. They had exhausted all possibilities. There was nothing more they could do. The father suddenly felt as if he were sitting before a doctor, not a policeman, that some mistake in the narrative had led him to the wrong place, that the plot had got mislaid somewhere, that he was, in fact, in a hospital corridor, not in a room with that superintendent.

"So you're saying there's no way of knowing –" Carmen spoke as if her voice was about to break, as if she might burst into tears on the next syllable – "if my son is alive or dead."

The superintendent sighed almost impatiently, but did not

69

avoid her gaze. His eyes seemed accustomed to such afternoons, having seen many people receiving the worst possible news.

"I think it would be best to assume that your son is dead, *señora*."

The three flinched. They had been over and over this possibility, but hearing it converted into one brief, laconic sentence uttered with such coolness sent a shudder down their spines. Rincón began to talk statistics.

"Last year there were more than thirteen thousand murders in the country as a whole," he said. "This year, there will be even more. In Caracas alone, there's an average of fifty a week. Most are the result of fights or quarrels in working-class areas, but there are a lot of stray bullets too, you understand."

They certainly understood the implication behind his words, but preferred to ignore it.

Stray bullets: bullets that come and go, that fall where they shouldn't, that get diverted and enter the wrong bodies, uninvited. Bullets apparently fired by no-one. Bullets of unknown origin. Bullets on the loose. Gone astray. You have to be alert. It could happen to anyone.

Maybe that was the best hypothesis, the final conclusion. Henry had been hit by a stray bullet. It happens all the time. Every day. Every minute. Every so often.

"What this country needs is a Ministry of Stray Bullets," said the superintendent, standing up now, ready to bid them goodbye. "Because there are a lot of unexplained homicides here. A lot of random murders, you understand." He raised his eyebrows and gestured towards the door with his yellow fingers.

In two weeks' time it will be a year since Henry disappeared. Omar has finally phoned Virginia to say that they need to get together. A French producer has been in touch with him to discuss the possibility of making a documentary about Henry. But they want both of them to be involved. They want them face to face, talking, arguing. That's something they've never done. They've always rejected any proposals to hold such a meeting.

"It would be an exclusive," says Omar, when he tells her about the French producer's offer. "They realise that."

"What do you mean?"

"They're offering us a good price. It's all above board. It would be a contribution both to the organisation promoting my candidacy and to your radio programme. What do you think?"

Virginia has spent the whole weekend at home, thinking about it. When she moved, she felt that she was, in a way, betraying Henry. She was abandoning their home, leaving behind the apartment they had lived in together, inventing a new space for herself alone, without him. True, the furniture was the same. She slept in the same bed. And she had arranged her husband's clothes in the wardrobe just as before. Everything was ready for his return. As was she, each night, as she lay in bed.

But time will not be beaten. It leaves no-one untouched. With the passing months, her life changed, very slowly, without her even realising it. At what precise moment did Henry's clothes begin to be a nuisance, inanimate bodies hanging in the darkness?

When did she stop crying at night? When did she begin to touch herself again, to feel desire? One afternoon, after a meeting, she ended up in a cheap motel with her lawyer. She had never before had such furious, desperate sex. She tore off his clothes, licked him, bit him, asked him to enter her, now, quickly; she clasped him to her, dug her fingers into his buttocks, to control his thrusting, yes, harder, harder. Then she burst into tears. She didn't want to talk. She felt ashamed to be crying too. She took a shower. And the only reason she didn't leave alone was because they had both arrived in the same car. She suddenly felt afraid that if she went out into the street looking for a taxi, she might bump into a photographer on the hunt for a scoop.

Omar is here now. He has come to see her, as they agreed, in order to make a decision. The people in France call him every day. They need an answer as soon as possible. Things are still not easy between the two of them. Virginia doesn't even offer him a coffee.

"So have you come to a decision?"

"No, I keep changing my mind."

"Me too. I can't decide either, but I said I'd give them our answer tomorrow."

"It's almost the anniversary of his disappearance. They probably want to cash in on that."

"I suppose so."

There is a moment of awkward silence. Until a mobile phone rings. Virginia stands up and walks over to the balcony to answer it. It's a call from an N.G.O. which has worked for years with homeless people. A week ago, they started drawing up a new census of the city's homeless. They have news. Virginia listens, stunned. Omar looks at her in bewilderment, aware that something is going on. He, too, stands up.

"Under the motorway," says the voice, "near the city centre, there's a large community of homeless people. It has a high turn-over rate. We were there yesterday. We saw someone who could be your husband. He's a bit out of it and he hasn't said anything yet, he doesn't speak, but there are a lot of similarities. We genuinely think he's Henry Lucena."

Virginia needs air. She feels faint. She goes back into the living room and slumps down on the sofa. She can hardly speak, she burbles something or other, she doesn't know what to say, please, could you call me again in ten minutes or so? She hangs up. Omar is staring at her, utterly perplexed.

"What's happened?"

Virginia tells him. Omar slides down onto the sofa next to her. They sit there together, astonished, open-mouthed.

"I can't believe it," she murmurs after a pause.

"Nor can I."

The whirlwind of the last months suddenly stops. The air grows heavy. Neither of them can find anything to say. They are bereft of language. They don't know how to react. They stay sitting like this for a few more minutes. Until the phone rings again. Virginia and Omar look at each other. The small mobile phone continues to sing out, lying on the glass-topped table. All alone. She slowly reaches out and touches Omar's hand. Their fingers are icy cold.

"Perhaps it isn't him," she says.

"That's just what I was thinking. Perhaps it's a mistake."

Dogs

1

I press the button to go down to basement level 3, but the lift ignores me and goes up instead. For some reason I stare accusingly at the ceiling. But this often happens, I mean, looking for explanations where there are none.

Lifts don't usually have any particular destination. Why doesn't it stop at the second floor? Or at the seventh? It continues impassively up to the fifteenth. I'm in a foul mood. When the sil-very doors slide open, I see a woman with badly dyed hair. Beside her stands her daughter. Or so I assume. She's a young twenty-something, whose only charm consists in being a young twenty-something. I've spent far too long being a man. And while this may not teach you very much, it does at least provide you with plenty of practice. A glance is all I need to make a judgement: innocent eyes, small, firm breasts, tight buttocks, probably still a virgin. She's carrying a dog. It's a dark brown cairn terrier. I instinctively move back to allow them in. As the doors close, the girl gives me a slightly pitying look. Perhaps she thinks I'm afraid of the dog.

"Don't worry," she says, smiling, "he doesn't bite."

"He may not," I say rather too quickly, "but I do!"

Everything happens at firecracker speed. I can hardly believe what I've just said. My courage sticks to the roof my mouth. I'm filled by a terrible, uncontrollable rage. My saliva burns me. The girl has no time to react. She doesn't know how to. Her mother manages to hit me with her handbag. Both women are screaming now. The girl is crying too. I seize the dog. I grab it round the neck with my right hand and squeeze; then with my left hand and arm I hold down the rest of its body. The dog resists, but, with a passion I've never known before, I bite into its back. The dog gives a yelp that sounds like an old train screeching to a halt during some foreign winter. I feel its fur between my teeth. It's like sinking your mouth and tongue into a rough paste. I don't care. I chew. Its skin is thick and elastic. If it wasn't a dog, it would be an octopus. But I like octopus. And this is the first time I've ever bitten a dog.

2

I can't possibly tell Elisa about this, I thought. Best not. I wouldn't know how to explain what I was doing in that building. I can't tell her I went there looking for a job, because she doesn't even know I lost my old one. It all seems so ridiculous, so absurd. My life changed radically for what seems a very simple reason that can be expressed in just a few words. They were laying people off and I was one of them. It sounds so dull. They were laying people off and I was one of them. It lacks oomph. It's just a series of rather bland words with no vigour, no shock value. It's not like saying you've got cancer.

Anyway, I lost my job. Yet I still never thought this was something that could possibly happen to me. Initially, I felt angry, indignant, but after a while, all I felt was embarrassment. Terrible embarrassment. That's why I lied to Elisa. Because I felt too ashamed to go home and tell her I'd been sacked, kicked out, dumped. That first night, I was so shaken I found it hard to sleep. I'll tell her tomorrow, I kept thinking, clutching that promise to myself: I'll tell her tomorrow.

The days passed and still I said nothing. Every time I steeled myself to tell her, that awful feeling of ignominy would become a physical obstacle, as if my mouth had filled up with stones. I couldn't speak. It seems such an easy thing to say: Elisa, I've lost my job. Well, you know how it is, what with the economy in the state it's in. And in this shitty country of ours. It seems so easy, but it isn't. Not for me. I just couldn't say it. I would immediately remember the money we owed on the apartment. Or her high hopes for our future. Women always dream more than men. I know she'd like to get pregnant. And I know, too, that each day that passes only makes matters worse, that the longer I delay, the harder it will be. Silence makes for an awkward accomplice. And I don't know how to break that silence.

"How were things at the office today?" she asked one Wednesday evening. A perfectly normal question.

"Oh, not bad. You know, the usual," I replied.

*

But as time passed, this clearly wasn't enough. I began to fear that my terse replies would make her suspicious. I tried to be chattier, more forthcoming, and slowly, before I knew it, I found myself creating a whole non-existent routine. I would talk about life at the office, tell anecdotes, stories; I would lie about my former work colleagues. One night, for example, I told her that Big García's father was in hospital. Whatever put that idea in my head? I still don't know. But by the time I'd asked myself that question, I was already in the middle of the story. Yes, he had a heart attack, I said. I found it difficult at first, but then I became more confident in my ability to imagine and invent a different story every night. Yes, a heart attack. Terrible. It happened while he was about to have a bath. Can you believe it? The downstairs neighbour realised something was wrong when water started pouring down the stairs. They found him lying on the floor, naked, drooling and gasping for air. It was a miracle he survived. Poor García is distraught.

That's what usually happens: we become hostages to apparently unimportant things. So I ended up surrounded by the stories I had invented in order to distract Elisa. I would set off to work each morning and, each night, I'd come home with a different tale, or with a new chapter to add to the great fiction that was my working life. I invented a life I no longer had, a life I had lost. In fact, I had all the time in the world to do nothing. At first, I went looking for another job, I phoned various companies, visited others, but with no success, no-one took me on. I began to spend

78

the days wandering the streets, kicking my heels, waiting until it was time to go home.

It was then that I first began to take a particular interest in dogs. I don't know why. But slowly I began to feel a curiosity, an appetite for all things canine. I noticed more dogs in the streets, was more aware of them, I even stopped to look in pet-shop windows. Suddenly, that curiosity, that appetite became a strange disquiet.

I had never liked dogs. On the contrary. I hated their complete absence of pride. I couldn't bear their servility, their joyful resignation, their astonishing lack of any sense of dignity. A dog can allow itself to be beaten by its master and still be happy, wagging its tail, begging for a little attention, to be stroked. A dog is cowed by its own need for affection, eternally pleading to be loved and wanted, to be given a chance.

That, at least, is what I had always thought, but suddenly I found myself salivating anxiously whenever a stray dog happened to pass by. One evening, when I watched a neighbour out walking his pooch, I was filled with a potent excitement. I tried to deny this to myself, but I couldn't: disquiet had become desire. I wanted to enter into close contact with dogs, with lots of them, with all of them. I wanted to bite dogs. To chew them. Just the thought made me tremble.

Desire can prove very uncomfortable. And very persistent.

3

These are some of the dogs I dream about: the Bernese mountain dog, with its abundant soft black hair, especially on its tail. Then there's the Japanese Akita, with its small eyes, rather like a domesticated wolf. The German wire-haired pointer, always restless and ready to race off. The Italian mastiff with its square, lordly head. The dachshund. The Catalan sheepdog, which is, of course, French. The Irish setter with its sad eyes. The Newfoundland with its equally melancholy gaze. I've never felt drawn to collies, although I find their thick hair seductive. The Hungarian Mudi is an interesting size. I'd like to try a dingo as well, a Brazilian or a Bordeaux mastiff. And a nice chunky bulldog never goes amiss. Ah, but there is nothing like the innocence of a golden retriever in the early hours of the morning.

4

That first time I did it in a lift, with a cairn terrier, which is not even a breed that interests me. That's what so often happens. Your first time can be with anyone, just to get it over with, more out of haste than taste; driven more by one's own ghosts than by the other body or what the other body may want. The first time, I was really frightened. I experienced a pleasure that quickly ceased to be pleasure and began to turn into fear: two entirely different sensations. I had to run away. Then I spent a few days feeling confused and vulnerable and racked with guilt. When I walked down the street, I was convinced that everyone who looked at me knew, that there was something about me that gave me away and that I couldn't hide. As if remnants of my sin still clung to my chin, as if my lips were stained with the dog's blood and hair. Even if no-one else could see them, they were there. That's how I felt. Crimes always leave a trail.

After a while, I calmed down. I found it very hard to accept what was happening to me, what I felt. It wasn't easy to acknowledge my desires. But it was too late to stop; I had taken the first step. At first, I was perhaps too cautious, trying out this new relationship only on stray dogs. They were easy enough to seduce. Ownerless dogs tend to be a pushover, always so eager for affection. I soon tired of them, however. They were too predictable, too keen, prepared to put up with anything, accustomed to being hurt. That wasn't what I was looking for.

I began to take more and more risks. All the time. Until I reached a marvellous kind of clandestinity. This lasted only a few days, but they were days filled with a kind of effervescent euphoria. The immense power of the forbidden drew me into committing various acts of madness. One morning, I went to the east of the city and stole a dog someone had left tied up outside a bank. She was a docile old chihuahua. Her hair was already stiff, almost crunchy, brittle. I took her to a derelict warehouse and shut myself up inside with her. I bit her several times. I also gnawed at one of her ears with my teeth. By the end, we were both of us out of breath, she more than me. She was in a desperate state. I don't think she could see me very well. She had cataracts.

After a few similar experiences, I tired of that too, grew weary of the air of illegality surrounding my relationship with dogs. I've no talent for it. I didn't like having to hide away like that, like a fugitive. As if I had a lover.

I spent nearly two weeks in a painful state of abstinence. I did a lot of thinking. I concluded that the world is not made for people who want to bite dogs in public. That was the problem. Then I devoted myself to observing how other people behave, and tried to analyse what was going on around me. I couldn't be the only one. It couldn't be happening to me alone. After careful observation, I discovered that I was right. There are lots of people like me. Loads of them. But they don't live as if their whole life were a crime. They conceal their true nature. That is the secret of happiness.

Almost everyone who has a dog tries to deal with the same desires I have. They keep their favourite animal at home. They feed it. They take it out for walks. They lead a perfectly natural and satisfactory social life. When they're with other people, they keep up the pretence that they have an entirely innocent and cordial relationship with their beloved mascot. But that's just a front. Intimacy always implies a victim. At some point, those people will finally show their true selves. They are fierce. And cruel. And they inflict harm. In the safety of their homes, when no-one is watching, I'm sure they bite their dogs. Pitilessly. Until they draw blood. Preferably at night. Darkness conceals even feelings of remorse.

*

In every city, every night, you can always hear a dog barking somewhere.

5

Today Big García told me that there could be a job for me this week. A vacancy has come up. Perhaps they'll give me another chance. He's going to do everything he can to get them to take me back. This evening, I told Elisa that García's father was better. They put a stent in, I said. They gave him a pacemaker too, and he's recovering well.

"García's feeling much more hopeful," I said.

To celebrate, I went to the pet shop and bought a dog. An American cocker spaniel. I paid for him with what remained of my redundancy money. I have a feeling things are going to go well for us, I said to Elisa. Besides, a mascot always brings good luck. He's a beautiful dog. With a very soft coat. We haven't given him a name yet.

A Sentimental Matter

Emilio Arcaya had lived alone ever since his wife left him to try her luck in Miami. His wife's name was Gisela. Presumably it still is. But that's what happens when someone leaves or goes away: they're left frozen in the past and can only be conjugated in the past tense. Gisela exited from this story a long time ago. All that remains are those few bleak words: she left her husband to try her luck in Miami. She didn't leave him for a Pedro or a Fernando, for a Ricardo or a Juan Carlos. She left him to go to southern Florida, to seek her fortune. Now that is true promiscuity.

Every night since, Emilio had religiously followed the same route from his apartment to the Oasis, a narrow little bar on the corner of Avenida Fuerzas Armadas, where, with elbows resting on the bar, he would sit drinking a glass of rum with three ice cubes in it. The bar was never anything very special. And it remained like that thanks to faithful customers like him. Nothing out of the ordinary ever happened, every day was the same, even as regards the kind and number of drinks each customer drank. Until the night Emilio walked into the bar and saw her and her wild mane of too-black, tar-black hair. She was sitting alone. Her skin had a blurred, distant pallor, as if she had spent years locked inside a wardrobe. Even Bruno, the eternal barman, seemed to have cast off his boredom. He wore a mischievous smile. Emilio eyed the stranger rather suspiciously. As he approached her, he took out a cigarette and lit it with a large, overly theatrical gesture. He sat down next to the young woman, attempting a smile. Bruno served him his usual rum on the rocks. The woman didn't even look at Emilio. Why should she? The yellow smoke from his cigarette stung her eyes. She moved away a little, stuck her finger in her glass and scratched the back of an ice cube.

"Would you like a drink?" He, of course, had to ask some such question.

The young woman didn't even blink in response. Emilio sensed that the battle was lost. She remained silent for a few seconds, but still continued that troubling movement with her finger. The ice cube would be submerged in the liquid, pushed gently downwards by her fingernail. Then it would bob back up, only to be submerged again, getting smaller and smaller, losing strength, size and vigour. The girl also kept her gaze fixed on the ice cube. She stuck out her tongue a little, ran it over her lips, then withdrew it. Suddenly, just as Emilio was about to surrender to the ochre charms of his rum, he was shaken by a sudden movement. The young woman next to him had sprung to her feet and was staring, terrified, at the door. Two burly men had entered. Emilio didn't know how he should react. The woman fled towards the back door of the bar. Emilio was aware only of her fleeing hips striking the shadows as she ran. When the door opened, a sliver of light allowed him to see other bodies grabbing hold of her and dragging her away. Her eyes seemed to reach out to him, and she screamed, as if begging him to come to her aid. It was a cry for help. Emilio ran, stumbled, fell, got up and again began running. By the time he had emerged from the rear door of the bar and found himself in the alleyway, it was already too late. All he could see were the headlights of a car as it turned the corner with a squeal of brakes, leaving only a disembodied scream echoing through the darkness.

Very gingerly he approached the corner. The darkness there was so thick, he felt as if he had to push his way through it; an all too familiar feeling. He found little of interest in the road: a syringe, a few rubbish bags, a cracked washbasin and a hand. Emilio stopped, bent down and studied the hand. Yes, it *was* a hand. Still warm. A woman's hand, covered in blood. Lying there. Gazing at the sky. Open, slender, alone, separated from its body. Emilio looked up and down the street, took out his handkerchief, quickly wrapped this around the hand and put it in his jacket pocket. He went back to the bar and, without a word of explanation, ordered another rum. And no ice, please.

When he woke up, the sun was already a tobacco-coloured pustule peering in at his window. He concocted a breakfast out of finely chopped sweet peppers and tomatoes and what remained of the contents of a carton of yoghurt. He looked hard at the photo of Gisela on the wall. It was an old black-and-white photo. Gisela was smiling. Emilio slowly unpinned it and put it away in a drawer. Then he opened the fridge and took out the hand, still wrapped in the handkerchief.

On the table, the hand looked somehow too white. The cold had stopped the blood. The small veins had swollen up and resembled green worms beneath the skin. Emilio picked up the phone and very slowly dialled a number.

"Operator 324."

"I need some information." Emilio wiped a drop of yoghurt from the sleeve of his shirt. "I've found a hand. It was probably reported missing last night."

"Are you making a complaint?"

"No, I just need some information."

"Which hand is it?" The voice sounded brusque and impatient. "Left or right?"

Emilio looked at the hand. He picked it up. It was beginning to grow warmer in the morning sunshine. Two drops of water glistened on the wooden tabletop.

"Left," he said at last, having pondered the shape of the fingers, while at the other end of the line he heard the operator tapping on the keyboard.

"No hand was reported missing last night. Sorry," said the voice after a pause.

And she hung up.

He had never liked asking his brother Esteban for help. Out of pride more than anything. In a way, Esteban was his role model, the successful brother Emilio was not and never would be. He always felt that, compared to Esteban, his life was a failure. At family reunions, Esteban always had some exploit to recount or some juicy bit of first-hand gossip or privileged information to share; he was so charming, so witty. He had prestige. He also had a job. He also had a wife. Beside him, Emilio was like a glaring absence, a sketch, a scribble, carelessly doodled on the air in a moment of tedium. And yet there he was, amazed at his own audacity, determinedly going up the steps to the main police station.

Esteban received him in a small office, wearing his usual expression, half-pleasure, half-disdain. Impeccable. Officer Arcaya. Homicide Department. With his shoulder holster on. Elegant but alert, and always ready for any emergency.

"Are you in trouble?"

"No, I just need your help."

Esteban sat down and studied him as suspiciously as only a career policeman can.

"That doesn't answer my question. Are you in trouble?" he asked again in a strangely emphatic way, singling out each word.

"I need to check the records."

"The records?" Esteban gave a resigned, impatient sigh. "What have you lost?"

"Nothing." He hesitated. "It's a purely sentimental matter."

Esteban stared at him, bemused. Then one corner of his mouth twitched into the suggestion of a smile.

"What have you got?"

"A hand."

Emilio placed the handkerchief on the desk. Esteban looked at it.

"It's quite fresh," Emilio added timidly, while Esteban drew back the edges of the handkerchief. "I found it last night."

They both sat there for a few seconds looking at it.

"At least you know she isn't black," Esteban commented at last.

Emilio didn't answer. He continued to observe Esteban, who had begun moving the hand around.

"That was a joke, Emilio. You're supposed to laugh." Esteban put his nose close to the hand and sniffed. Then he looked in detail at the fingertips. "No cocaine. That's a shame. No rings either. That would have been ideal, you know. Rings sometimes have dates and names engraved on them."

Emilio had a bad feeling. He felt suddenly that it had been a mistake to come here.

"Do you know the woman?"

"I think so."

"Ah, always the same precise, confident Emilio," said Esteban with heavy irony. "I hope she isn't another disaster area like that whore you married. Heard anything from *her* lately?"

"She's still in Miami."

"You don't like to talk about it, do you?"

"Could you please just check the records?"

Esteban sighed. He ordered Emilio to close the door, then turned on his computer, opened the lid of the scanner and placed the hand on the glass screen.

"Let's see now." He began tapping rapidly on the keyboard. "I spoke to the old girl yesterday. She said she hasn't heard a word from you in weeks. She's left you several messages."

"I know."

"You should call her, even if it's really late. She doesn't ask so many questions then."

Emilio was still staring at the screen. Then a few tremulous yellow letters appeared.

"No, there's no match. No file. Nothing. The woman doesn't exist."

Emilio went out into the evening, filled with a sense of unease. He had lunched on a measly bit of bread with ham and cheese. Then he had drunk two cups of coffee and trudged into town. This route inevitably reminded him of the days immediately following Gisela's disappearance, when he had felt unable to settle anywhere, filled by an urgent need to be constantly on the move. Going nowhere, but never stopping. He had spent whole days wandering, never arriving anywhere, never finding anything. What he had most wanted then was to have no head at all, and he walked from one place to another simply in order not to think. Not thinking is a very difficult thing to achieve. Not thinking is an art.

Now he found himself on a bench in a square. He put the handkerchief on his lap and very slowly lifted the corners as if he were unwrapping a sandwich. Then he contemplated the hand for a few moments. He pondered the memory contained in bodies. If only that hand could talk, could tell him what it lacked, could speak to him out of its absence. Bodies have a different kind of wisdom, a different logic. They see death more clearly. They know death. They know it before we do. They can hear its creeping footsteps inside them. They speak to it. They negotiate. We may not even sense its presence, but our bodies know when death is near. Emilio placed his own hand on the one resting on the handkerchief. Finger on finger. Palm on palm. Fingerprint on fingerprint. The coldness of that other skin made him shudder slightly. What would that hand say to him now? What memories would still be beating beneath those stiff, cold fingers? Where would that hand take him? What direction was it pointing in?

It was only when he saw his reflection, his blurred image in the opaque glass of the door, that he realised he was back in the same place. He rang again. It was a small shop selling esoterica. It sold herbs and potions too, as well as candles and altars and figures from various religions. A poster announced that on Thursday afternoons, they offered tobaccomancy, reading the ash on a client's cigarette or cigar. Lower down, in smaller print, mentioning no specific day or hour, it said: "Injections given." It was nearly dark. Emilio was about to give up when, at last, the door opened. Nothing really changes very much. There was the old woman. The same as always. She seemed frozen in time. Swathed in brightly coloured fabrics. Grubby even in her gestures.

"Oh, it's you again," she said.

Emilio sat down on the stool next to the table.

"Have you got money with you?"

"Yes."

Emilio produced the hand wrapped in the handkerchief and gently placed it on the table.

"Why have you come?"

"To have a palm read," he murmured.

The old woman opened her lips slightly: a solitary tooth seemed to dance about on her dry breath.

"Don't be a smart-arse. Give me the money."

He took three green notes from his wallet and handed them to her. She nodded.

"Did you bring some drink too?"

"No."

The old woman bent down and picked up a large dark bottle. In one movement, she raised it to her lips and drank.

"It's only cheap stuff, but it'll do," she said. "So," she added, tugging at the corners of the handkerchief, "you've found a hand."

"How do you know I didn't steal it?"

The old woman didn't even deign to look at him. With some difficulty, she straightened out each finger until the hand lay flat.

"What do you want to know?"

"I'm looking for a woman."

"The same one as before?"

"No."

She blew twice on the palms of her own hands and returned to her task. Suddenly, a finger creaked. She pressed down on it with her knuckles, trying to straighten it out.

"Does this hand belong to the woman you're looking for?"

"I think so."

She began to knead the hand. The tip of her tongue appeared between her lips. Dark and blotchy. Like octopus blood. She was making rapid movements now, accompanied by incomprehensible murmurings. Emilio thought she was talking – if, that is, she *was* talking – in another language. Or perhaps she was merely repeating sounds devoid of all logic or sense.

Beneath her fingers, the hand resembled a rather awkward toy. She kept pressing harder, although it was clear she was getting nowhere. The hand would not soften. It remained tense and unyielding.

"I'm not going to be able to read it while it's in this state," she said. "It's too stiff."

"Oh, come off it."

"No, I'm serious. The hand won't cooperate."

Emilio got angrily to his feet. He picked up the handkerchief.

"Give me back my money."

She hunched still further over the hand, refusing to release it.

"No, I won't. I'm doing my best, but, like I said, it's not cooperating."

They both looked at each other for a second. An insect suddenly flew into one of the candles. A small fly perhaps. Too close. A crackle of wings. Gone.

"This hand will only bring you trouble. You should throw it in the river."

Emilio looked at her, trying and failing to appear sceptical. His suspicions were easily assuaged. Basically, he was prepared to hear whatever she had to tell him, regardless of what it was.

"And the woman I'm looking for?"

"Forget her. Besides, you're wrong. She isn't a different woman.

She's the same one, the one you've always been looking for."

After a brief moment of hesitation, Emilio was gripped by rage. His throat felt as if it were full of tiny raw creatures. Anger made him shift anxiously from side to side, almost hopping from foot to foot. He wrung his hands. He stammered a few words. Then he fixed the old woman with a look of deep, penetrating loathing. She took refuge from his gaze in drink, taking another swig from the bottle. Emilio felt like killing her. Stupid old bag; not that she was to blame, of course. It might be a relief though. This was the first time in a long while that he had experienced a real urge to do something. And the sudden impulse to kill someone changed something in him, and he was filled by a rare feeling of calm. He picked up the hand and the handkerchief and left without saying another word.

He went back to the bar. He had his right hand deep in his jacket pocket, clutching the other hand. Fingertips touching fingertips, stroking the nails, the palm. Perhaps that's why it felt less cold. As soon as he entered the bar, he looked around expectantly. He was hoping to find the same girl there again. Exactly the same: leaning on the bar, staring into a glass with a few ice cubes floating around in it. Exactly the same: tar-black hair, skin as pale as if she had spent years locked inside a cupboard. But she wasn't there.

He stayed on into the early hours. Waiting. Waiting for her. Bruno served him a series of drinks with and without ice. Emilio definitely wanted to die. There are those intent on dying of love, but whom love will not oblige. At closing time, Emilio asked for one last drink in a plastic cup and left reluctantly by the back door that led out into the alleyway. Nothing had changed: shadows, the odd syringe, detritus. He stood with his back to the wall and slid down until he felt the icy chill of the pavement on his buttocks.

A ray of sunlight startled him awake, the heat almost pressing itself against his cheek. He eased open his eyelids. His tongue felt like sandpaper, his head as if it were filled with liquid lead. He was lying down surrounded by litter. He had the impression that he'd woken up inside someone else's stomach. He managed to roll over onto his hands and knees. A cat appeared before him. A huge ginger cat. It had the hand in its mouth. Or, rather, like a hunting dog with its prey, it had one finger between its teeth, and the rest of the hand was dragging limply along the tarmac. Emilio stared at it in amazement. He tried to get closer, crawling on all fours. He bent forward and attempted a miaow. An indescribable sound emerged from his lips. A string of collapsed vowels. A pathetic, saliva-filled howl. The cat took fright and, still without letting go of the hand, bounded away. Emilio could not stop it. He stumbled and fell. When he got up again, cat and hand were only a blur, a faint gleam at the end of the alleyway.

Famous Writers

When Hugo Chávez became President of the Republic, our teacher, Batista, summoned us all to meet in the library that Tuesday night. Batista led a writing workshop in the Central University's Literature Department. He was tall and thin, but not bony as tall, thin people are usually said to be. He didn't smoke either. Or drink or have any success with girls. And it wasn't just a gender issue – Batista wasn't popular with any section of the student population. He was a complete and utter failure. Not even literature could save him. That semester, ten students had enrolled for the workshop, but by the time of the meeting on that Tuesday night, only five of us were left.

"Do you want to become famous writers?" he asked.

No-one knew what to say. No-one knew why he was asking the question. Jorge and I looked at each other, equally confused. Basically, I think we felt intimidated. There we were, eighteen-year-old shrimps with little experience, mere about-to-bes in our first year at university. And yet Batista insisted: Why were we there? Did we or did we not want to become famous writers?

We all immediately said that we did, like children asked to explain some difficult word and afraid of being found out.

*

In the country's strange new political situation, Batista saw a marvellous passport, a direct route to possible literary glory. According to his calculations, sooner or later the Bolivarian revolution would oblige the world to turn its fickle eyes on Venezuela. Our moment had finally arrived. We should immediately start writing stories of defiant resistance, dramatic tales of persecuted Latin Americans, stories imbued with a feisty heroism locked in permanent battle with the totalitarian threat. We must revisit the tension between private and historical tragedy, he said, or words to that effect. Have any of you read Marina Tsvetaeva? I'll bring in one of her books to show you. Batista's enthusiasm was rock solid. He believed firmly that we should follow the Cuban example. I'm not talking about Cabrera Infante or Reinaldo Arenas, but about the endless numbers of third-rate scribblers who, thanks to Fidel Castro, are living in Miami, Berlin or Barcelona. Don't you see? This is our moment! A once-in-a-lifetime opportunity!

At first, Jorge and I thought the man had gone mad. I had met Jorge on the very first day of the semester. He was the one who told me about the writing group. According to Jorge, Batista had not had much luck as a writer. He wasn't well known. Ten years ago, he'd won a short-story competition in the provinces somewhere. He'd had a novel published too, but, fortunately for readers, or so Jorge said, this had gone virtually unnoticed. And yet he was often to be seen on the judging panels of literary prizes. Jorge had his own theory about this. Batista tended to fill his texts with quotes from the classics. As if, rather than actually writing anything, he wanted to demonstrate how very cultivated he was. That's what Jorge said anyway. His stories were always full of allusions to important authors and to major works of world literature. Batista wrote sentences like this: "And then Andrés Camejo suddenly felt just as Laurence Sterne did when he arrived in Calais." In this way, he gradually began to gain a reputation as the formidably well-read master of a vast and luxuriant culture, the ideal person to be a competition judge.

That night, after the meeting with Batista, Jorge and I went for a drink. We usually frequented one of the hostess bars near the old bus station, on the fringes of the city centre. Jorge loved these awful places. I'm just being honest, he would say, ordering another beer and another pack of cigarettes. Then he would add with a smile: After all, this is what we deserve, isn't it? In those days, no-one talked about anything but politics. Politics poisoned the whole country. Jorge thought Chávez was a fraud, a clown. I, on the other hand, had voted for him in the elections. I believed in his diatribes against corruption, against privilege. How was it that in such a rich country more than 60 per cent of the population continued to live in poverty? He's just the same as all the others, said Jorge, you'll see. Oh, don't be such a prat, I would say. The dawn found us abandoning our debate and looking instead at two of the women who worked in the bar. They had gone into the toilet, leaving the door open. There they were, half-sitting or crouching around the toilet bowl, almost embracing each other, both of them completely plastered. It wasn't easy to tell what they were doing there. Perhaps one of them had just been sick. They both seemed well under the influence. We couldn't tell either if they were laughing or crying, or if they were laughing and crying at the same time. One was short and dumpy. She was wearing black shorts and a pair of cheap boots. The other was dark-skinned, and yet I remember her as being very pale, perhaps because she was feeling ill. She had curly hair and a melancholy smile. Outside, sitting at the bar, a sour-faced man was waiting for them. He looked absolutely furious and demonstrated his impatience by repeatedly slamming a beer bottle down on the counter. He was shouting something at them, but I can't remember what. The two women ignored him completely. They sometimes grabbed each other's hands and bent forwards beneath the stark light of the bare bulb hanging from the ceiling. But they showed no intention of getting up and joining the man waiting for them. They stayed there, their bottoms on the cold floor, swaying about like two weary, drunken walruses.

At one point, the dumpy one turned her head and noticed us for the first time. From her position, with the toilet door open, it was as if our table had suddenly swum into her field of vision. With something resembling a smile, she asked if we could give her a cigarette. That one simple request was all it took for the sour-faced man to knock over his bottle, shout some abusive comment and take out a pistol. I leapt to my feet, although I really don't know why. I wasn't intending to fight him. Perhaps I was just getting ready to run away, but I didn't do that either. I stood there, staring at the bottles of rum on the shelf behind the bar, while the manager and another man tried to calm the situation down. The two women were laughing or crying or embracing, their elbows resting on the edge of the toilet bowl.

"Do you think this is how you're going to get to be a famous writer?" asked Jorge, chuckling, as we emerged from the bar into the night.

A few weeks later, Batista was putting together our future book, an anthology of combative Venezuelan stories. We were already the country's future dissident writers. We would all be included, that is the five of us who were still members of the workshop, as well as Batista himself, who assured us that he was working on a couple of stories himself. He was still fired up with enthusiasm, although he did ask us to be discreet: We don't want someone stealing our idea, do we? Batista arrived at each class with vast quantities of material with which to feed our imaginations. Have you seen what the newspapers are saying? Did anyone listen to last night's speech? Five hours, dammit! He was talking for five whole hours! Now here's a good subject: Chávez has made so many trips abroad that, this year alone, they reckon he's been around the world three times. That's not a revolution! That's just a sheer waste of petrol! Now I wouldn't want to impose my views on you – it's just a suggestion – but whenever the president says that anyone who isn't with him is against him, I can't help thinking of the great Latin American tradition of novels about dictators. Just a suggestion.

And almost all of us began writing stories based on our

teacher's suggestions. Batista was overjoyed. Until, one afternoon, Jorge said he'd had enough, that he just wanted to write a personal story, a family anecdote that had nothing to do with present-day reality. Batista's enthusiasm visibly crumpled. Jorge pretended not to notice. He said he wanted to write about his grandfather.

He was nearly eighty, in poor health and extremely bad-tempered. It was a simple story, Jorge said. Over the years, his grandfather had gradually grown distrustful and suspicious of everything: of the climate and the neighbours, of vegetables and the television, of his own children and himself. He saw danger lurking everywhere, in the slightest gesture, the smallest incident. This sense of dread had caused him to develop an unhealthy relationship with money, the little money he had. He was so obsessed that he made a daily trip to the bank near his house, to make sure that his savings were still there, in the account provided by Social Security. None of the family could convince him that this was pointless and ridiculous. Indeed, their efforts only made matters worse, because he began to suspect that they had some dark ulterior motive for trying to stop him going to the bank. Occasionally, he made the same trip several times a day. Jorge's mother was growing increasingly concerned about this. Perhaps that's why she assigned Jorge the task of accompanying his grandfather on these "business trips". They would come and go together, part of a silent routine. The old man would enter the bank and hand over his savings book. Day after day, the same thing. Day after day, the employees would update his book, assuring him that his money was still there. It was impossible to persuade him that this operation was quite unnecessary, that there was no need to do it every single day. Reassured and smiling, Jorge's grandfather would merely say: Bye. See you tomorrow.

Batista tried to change Jorge's story. He always had some criticism to make, picking him up on his use of a particular adjective or some perceived flaw in the motivation of one of his characters. He felt that the story lacked "bite", that it was rather flabby in comparison with what the rest of us were writing. Jorge listened attentively to his remarks, but took not a blind bit of notice. The following week, he would read us a new section of his story, which incorporated none of Batista's suggestions.

The story reached a climax on the afternoon when grandson and grandfather paused outside a new addition to the bank – a small space, with glass walls, behind which there were four cash dispensers. These were already being used by customers, and the grandfather was watching with great interest. He was also highly suspicious, never having had much faith in such machines. He consulted his grandson and grumbled a bit, while the boy tried to win him over to the wonders of technology. And yet what really seemed to fascinate the grandfather was the transparent design of the place, the glass walls, the natural lighting. From that moment on, the grandfather's routine began to change. He became increasingly interested in the cash dispensers. He stopped going into the bank to check his balance and, instead, began to spend long periods of time inside the glass box. He now checked his balance on one of the machines, always the same one, and then he would linger there, wandering about, observing the other customers. His grandson, in turn, observed him from outside. The old man gradually developed the strange habit of checking other people's receipts. He would pick up the bits of paper the other customers had dropped on the floor or deposited in the bin provided. He did so discreetly, trying to disguise his intentions with all kinds of superfluous gestures, but always ended up doing the same thing – picking up a piece of paper and reading it rapidly, avidly. Sometimes he would smile. Sometimes he would throw the receipt down on the ground almost angrily. Sometimes he would carefully fold it up and put it away in one of his trouser pockets. There were occasions, too, when he would look at his grandson through the glass wall and gently raise one hand, asking for a little more time. I won't be long, he was saying. Just a moment longer.

When Jorge finished reading his story, we sat in silence for a few moments. Eugenia, a girl in her sixth semester, asked if the story was true, if his grandfather was still alive and if he was like the man in the story, if he had based his story on real people and events. Jorge wouldn't be drawn. Somewhat awkwardly, Batista spoke then about the reality on which all literary works are based. What country does this story take place in? he asked, as if addressing no-one in particular. When does it take place? At what point in history? The present day? None of us broke the silence. Perhaps all our hands were sweating. You could feel it. Or something like it. As if the air itself were sweating.

"What connection, for example," asked Batista, finally looking straight at Jorge, "what connection does your story have with what is going on in this country right now?"

"None," answered Jorge. "My grandfather doesn't even know what country he's living in."

No anthology of combative Venezuelan stories was ever published. The semester ended and things went on as before. Batista left the university or perhaps, who knows, he was fired. I heard nothing more of him until four years later, after Jorge's funeral.

The headline read: "One dead and two injured in an attack on a bus." It happened just before 10.00 at night, on a bus travelling the El Llanito–La Pastora route. Witnesses say that it happened very fast, too fast. The assailants were four boys. They were high on drugs. One was carrying a sawn-off shotgun. One passenger refused to give up his watch, and that was when things turned nasty. The boys got angry, you know how it is. It was just awful. Then a man at the back of the bus stood up and started shouting. Another passenger, a young man, came forward and tried to calm things down, but it was no use, it all ended in tragedy. There was blood everywhere. I didn't know the two injured men. Jorge was dead on arrival at hospital.

After that workshop, Jorge and I had somehow never coincided on any of the same courses. We remained friends, but we didn't see each other so much. Not that this diminished the shock and pain of his death. I was one of the few friends who had met his mother and one of his sisters. At the undertaker's, I went over to them and offered my condolences on behalf of all the other students. At the cemetery, when the coffin was being lowered into the grave, Jorge's mother fell to her knees on the dry grass. She started shouting. No-one could really understand what she was saying. Perhaps she wasn't saying anything. I bowed my head so as not to have to look at her.

A few days later, a group of us students met in room 209. We had all been friends of Jorge. Some more than others. We could still not take in what had happened. We were angry and upset; we felt so powerless, we couldn't accept that life was merely a game of chance: tomorrow it could be you or him or anyone. That afternoon we read Jorge's story, each of us reading a section out loud.

I read the part where the grandfather began picking up the receipts other customers had dropped on the ground or placed in the litter bin. My voice quavered slightly when I got to the bit where the old man would rush off to the metro station, clutching those bits of paper. At the end, someone said that Jorge was clearly destined to become a famous writer.

Not long after his death, it was announced in the newspapers that Batista was publishing a collection of short stories. A photo of him – tall and thin, but not bony – appeared on the front page of the review sections. He had clearly stuck to his goal, because the book was called *Days of Blood*. The headline announced that these were "Stories from a country engaged in defiant resistance". The launch was to take place on a Friday night, at one of the major bookshops. Asdrúbal Martínez, the leader of a grass-roots organisation opposed to the government, would be introducing the book. I arrived early. I don't really know why I went. I felt uncomfortable about it, but curiosity got the better of me. There was already quite a crowd. It was a pretty lavish affair with waiters, a long table groaning with bottles of wine and canapés; and cameras from two television channels were there too. On a stand in one corner of the shop, small piles of books had been arranged around a poster that echoed the headline: "Stories from a country engaged in defiant resistance". I picked up a copy and leafed rapidly through it, as if sampling each title, each opening line. Until I reached the seventh story, entitled "In the Red". It was the story Jorge had written about his grandfather going to the bank every day and getting becalmed in that fishbowl full of cash machines and bits of paper. I just couldn't believe it. Batista had even changed the ending: grandson and grandfather go on the famous march against the government that took place on 11 April 2002. I read the story quickly and with growing astonishment. Grandson and grandfather walk through the city centre, in an act of peaceful protest. Grandson and grandfather are suddenly struck down by bullets coming from a group of sharpshooters supposedly hired by the government. Grandson and grandfather die together in the street. *Prohibido olvidar.* Never forget!

I almost dropped the book. Like a stone. I was paralysed. I didn't know what to do. I looked around for Batista. He was nowhere to be seen. I felt utterly empty. I left. The night hung over the city like a thin layer of rust.

I took a taxi, not really knowing where I was going. I just

wanted to drift, to drive around for hours and hours, never stopping, never reaching a destination. Finally, though, I had to make a decision. Half an hour later, I found myself in that same hostess bar, on the fringes of the city, near the old bus terminal, sitting at the same table where Jorge and I used to sit in the days when we were still attending Batista's workshop. The place hadn't changed much. It was almost empty. There were scarcely any women. The jukebox was playing a dance tune – a *cumbia*. The door to the toilets was closed. There was no dumpy woman in shorts and cheap boots. No dark woman with pale skin. No sour-faced, impatient man waiting for them. Yet that was precisely what I wanted to see, what I was looking for. I wanted them to be there, brazenly drunk, sitting on the cold floor, their arms about the altar of the toilet bowl, vomiting, laughing or crying, or laughing and crying at the same time. I sat at the table as if waiting for the right moment, for some meaningless gesture, for someone to ask for a cigarette. Waiting to hear the screams of some hopeless man at the bar, waving a gun around; waiting to see a pair of drunken women starkly lit by a bare bulb. And me staring at the bottles of rum on the shelf. Me, alone, understanding nothing, not knowing what to do, not knowing whether to stay or flee, not knowing what country I was living in.

Last Night

Manuel doesn't know if it's a dream or a memory. All he can see is himself in the car park, crouched in front of his old Fiat. He looks dreadful: he's wearing a pair of faded jeans and a crumpled T-shirt. He's so pale he's almost white, as if he's been up all night or has just got out of bed. He's staring at a piece of cloth stuck to the front bumper. It seems to be a scrap of dirty fabric, torn from a pair of trousers and imprinted on the metal bumper. There's a large dark stain on the cloth. It appears to be blood. This can't be happening, he thinks. It must be a dream. If it were real, he would behave differently, he would at least stand up or respond more energetically. Why does he just stay there, crouched and staring, as if he wasn't even surprised? Why doesn't he try to peel off the piece of cloth? Why is he so inert? What is he waiting for?

The light hurts him. Even with his eyes closed, he can sense it out there, on the other side of his eyelids, touching, scratching, trying to get in. He wonders what time it is. It could be eight or nine or even eleven o'clock in the morning. Beyond his bed, the world is a precipice. Even the light is stumbling and dissolving, faltering and falling. When he finally opens his eyes, his lids snap shut. The brightness wounds them. It's not the alarm clock sounding, but the light. The light is a needle piercing his eye.

Everything else remains in shadow. Manuel can't tell if he's awake or still drunk. His head is full of soggy cardboard. He can't remember anything. Everything is pure hangover, pure morning-after-the-night-before.

A possible definition of a hangover: the breath dry, but at the same time viscous. Like urine-soaked sand. Everything carries with it the unbearable feeling of being covered in layer upon layer of dirt. Objects suddenly become crowds. Every gesture is preceded by a slight tremor. The classic cold sweat does precisely what a classic cold sweat should do. It's there on the palms of your hands, your forehead, bum, shoulders, lips . . . Your breathing is not really breathing. It's merely a victim of its own nausea. Then there's the anxiety. A secret, almost furtive anxiety that touches everything and leaves nothing unscathed. Depending on the circumstances – and the quality of the materials consumed – an impertinent headache sometimes appears out of nowhere and shrivels up all five known senses. Vomiting is an easy way out, but not entirely effective. The sense of biological shipwreck will take hours to disappear. Not even a beer on waking is enough. Not even a bowl of cereal swimming in vodka will do the trick. Nor will tomato juice. The hangover is an obligation that cannot be relieved by the application of more ice. It is the body returning. It's the inevitable day after, the certain knowledge that there is no-one left to fight with.

After taking a long pee, Manuel goes onto the balcony and leans out. From there, he can look down at his car, can check it exists, that it actually arrived, that it faithfully brought him home. He can only see the roof, the boot and the bonnet. From the eleventh floor, the bumper is invisible. Did it really happen or did I dream it? He can't quite locate that wretched piece of cloth. Where is it? In his memory or in his fear?

He's often had the same recurring nightmare: he's drunk at the wheel. The old Fiat is driving itself, it knows the way. The sun only came up a short while ago. It's seven o'clock or thereabouts. Suddenly, a boy appears around the corner, is there in front of him, running after a ball, sometimes fast, sometimes slow. Manuel doesn't have time to brake. Nor can he avoid him. There is no bash, no smash, no crash. It's more muffled than that. No harsh consonants. Like a drop of saliva falling into the ear. Just once. Manuel closes his eyes, but he can still see the boy flying briefly through the air. He doesn't hear him hit the road, but he knows that he has fallen, that he is there. The silence is frightening. Manuel doesn't dare look. He only opens his eyes again when he's sure he's far from that street and safe in his bed. Neither awake nor asleep. Somewhere halfway between sleep and imagination. Possibly still drunk.

He feels like that now, gazing down at the roof of his car. That scrap of stained cloth, stuck to his bumper, might just be a fragment from the bad dream he's still inhabiting, that has not let go, not yet vanished beneath the weight of the light. For a second, he gives in to the temptation to sit down and try to remember what he did last night. Nothing. His memory doesn't respond. The night is an empty wardrobe into which he ventures only to find nothing, hear nothing, not even the sound of his own footsteps. A lone image surfaces in his mind. A woman with short, tousled hair. She's laughing and drinking wine. She's smoking too. She might also be sniffing cocaine. She's wearing a sleeveless purple blouse. Her nipples, underneath the fabric, resemble the blank eyes of a toad. She is the one bright thing in that very murky place. Was that before or afterwards? There's the motorway. And a tall grey building that comes and goes. Could it be Avenida Victoria? Then nothing else, only the piece of cloth stuck to the bumper.

"I'm here, crouched down by the engine, right, and it's there in front of me. It's a piece of cloth, I'm sure of that," says Manuel. And he stretches out his hand to touch the fabric with the tip of one finger. He scratches it with his nail. "It looks like it came from a pair of trousers, do you get what I mean?"

Raúl does not. Perhaps he prefers not to. Manuel moves his hand, and shifts the phone to his other ear.

"Perhaps you're still drunk," comments Raúl.

"No, I'm not." Manuel glances from side to side and lowers his voice. "That's why I picked up my mobile and dialled your number. I just want you to tell me what happened last night."

"Don't you remember?" asks Raúl.

"No, I remember fuck all."

"Absolutely nothing?"

Raúl's house is the only thing that remains, in the background, behind or beneath many layers of opaque scales. He knows that last night he was supposed to be at Raúl's house at 10.00. That was the arrangement.

"We'll see you at ten o'clock here," he had said.

"O.K., ten o'clock at your place," said Manuel.

He manages to remove the piece of cloth with a pair of pliers. It's not easy. It's like a skin tattooed onto the metal. He doesn't like to think that there must also have been some liquid, some fluid that served as glue, that stuck the cloth to the bumper. The dark stain. He doesn't even want to imagine what he already is imagining. It must be blood.

He doesn't dare get into his car. In the taxi to Raúl's house, he looks anxiously out at the places they pass. Perhaps he's hoping that some detail will suddenly return his memories to him intact, that a single object will dispel the cloud of alcohol still floating inside his head. Is it possible to remain so utterly blank, as if that piece of the night had never existed, as if it had been erased for ever? As tends to happen, this question conceals another still more frightening one: what are we capable of doing when we're drunk, when we're out of control, when no-one is watching us, when even our memory cannot see us?

On one corner, he sees a man ferreting around among some rubbish bags. He's not particularly swarthy, but his skin seems dark, as if it were covered by a fine, firm layer of gelatine, as if he had painted his body with grime. No-one bothers to have a wash before going in search of possible treasures inside rubbish bags. It isn't a task that requires you to be well turned out or to wear a special uniform. You don't have to comb your hair. Manuel looks at him and thinks that the man is not a man, but a fly. "The shit that others leave behind is his food." For example, the leftovers from yesterday's supper. A small strip of chicken still attached to a bone, mixed with the contents of an ashtray and the floral softener you add when the washing machine reaches its third cycle. What does that smell like? What does it taste like? Manuel feels a wave of disgust. He doesn't want to see the man. He doesn't want to smell him. He doesn't even want to feel that they occupy the same stretch of road, that they are somehow together. He would prefer not to know that he exists; he would like to live in a state of total innocence, far from the man, far from their mutual rubbish; to live without pain, without repugnance.

He is assailed by another image: awash with vodka, at 3.00 in the morning, driving his old Fiat, he himself is passing that same corner. He's either coming from or going to – well, it doesn't really matter where. And then he sees the same man, his skin the same revolting colour. He's crossing the street, carrying a black plastic bag over his shoulder. The day's booty. He isn't so much walking as buzzing. He's a grubby, hairy insect. Manuel feels as if he were suffocating, everything around him is tinged with yellow. Gripped by terrible desperation, he doesn't stop, he presses down on the accelerator, driving ever faster. The man doesn't have time to react, and when he turns, he stands frozen in the headlights. The car hits him at 110 kilometres per hour.

Could he do that? Could Manuel actually do something like

that? Could he have done that last night, for example? Why not? After all, he wouldn't remember anything the next day. He might assume it was all just a dream, a vague dream. He could listen to the news on the radio without a flicker of emotion, he could hear how, once again, some homeless person had been run down, and still he would remember nothing. Like today. Like now.

By the time he reaches Raúl's house, he's trembling. He tries to light a cigarette, chokes, stubs it out, and asks for a glass of water. He's dizzy with anxiety. He doesn't talk to Raúl about his fears. He may not even want to or be able to put them into words. It's best to keep fear and language separate. But he's in such a state now that he needs to find out what happened last night. Raúl says: We were here until midnight, waiting for Chino to call and tell us if the party at Los Chaguaramos was on or not. Do you really not remember even that? O.K., calm down, it's not my fault if you don't. When Chino phoned and said there was nothing doing, you and I went to the Happy Club. We were there until about two o'clock. At least I was. That's where we met those two girls. What were their names now? One was Esther or something and the other one . . . was she called Dayana? I don't know. Anyway, you got it into your head that you'd scored with one of them, I can't remember which, the short one I think, the chubby one. You were drunk by then, so pissed you could hardly speak. I told you that over and over, but it was no use. That's why I left. I got fed up and left. That's all. That's all I can tell you, Manuel. The rest of the story is yours.

But Manuel has no rest of story. Well, he has a possibly blood-stained piece of cloth stuck to the bumper of his car. That's all the evidence that remains. He frowns, worried. Today, he doesn't like the word "evidence".

"You'll have to wait for the staff on the late shift to come on," says the man as he starts putting away the glasses. "I only work until eight," he adds.

Manuel has ordered a beer and confided in the barman, things he does far too often. There's a common fantasy that someone who has seen a lot of drunks from close up must be a wise man. People think that someone who listens to drunks all the time has some kind of special insight. It's only midday, and Manuel, leaning on the bar of the Happy Club, still doesn't know quite why he's there. Perhaps he's just beginning to experiment with different ways of doing penance.

"It happens a lot." The man continues talking as he pours his beer. "More than you might think. Every day, someone turns up here asking if they left their house keys or their wallet, or a new jacket, or their diary. They wake up and they can't remember a thing. What did *you* lose?"

Manuel would like to say that he's lost his memory, that he's mislaid a few hours from the previous night; or that what he's really lost is his peace of mind, because he suspects that, during the blank nothing that is his memory, he might have done something terrible, irrevocable, might have committed a crime. He would also like to say that all he lost was a clean bumper. That he's haunted by a wretched piece of stained cloth that keeps spinning around him, soiling his day and his words. It could be blood. And yet instead, after a pause, he invents some convoluted story in which two girls somehow end up with his address book and . . . In the middle of the story something resembling a memory appears. It's just a glimmer. It's his memory scratching at the door. A desperate gesture that fleetingly lights up his eyes. He sees a cheque. He sees one of the girls signing a cheque. An ice cube melting . . . then everything is plunged once more into darkness. Manuel attempts a still more tortuous route: perhaps the two girls paid with a cheque, he says, and since it's Sunday, he says, perhaps that cheque is still in the till. Perhaps, he insists, one of those girls might, as people usually do, have written her details on the back of the cheque: the number of her ID card and her phone number. Perhaps, he says again. This is a speculation full of twists and turns, but it might work. The barman looks at him in amazement. Manuel orders another beer and offers the barman a generous tip. More than a tip, it's a bribe. Or that, at least, is what Manuel thinks. And he doesn't care. It might also be considered a reward. He no longer cares what name he gives to his actions. He just wants to know if he is or isn't guilty of what happened, even though he still doesn't know what did actually happen.

While the barman checks the till receipts from the previous night, Manuel again sees the boy flying through the air. He feels dizzy. A boy running after a ball. He thinks about the homeless man as well. A man in pursuit of rubbish.

"Here it is," says the barman, coming over, holding a cheque. "This might be it. Esther González. Ring any bells?"

Manuel is now outside the door of apartment 32-C. The building is called Las Brisas and stands at the top of Avenida Urdaneta. He's about to ring the bell. He hesitates. Is this really necessary? He spoke to Esther on the phone. He lied to her as well, greeting her effusively as if they were still at last night's party. She replied wearily, possibly even grumpily. He told her: I've got a surprise for you. A surprise? she asked. Yes, he said, and she didn't know what to say. Then after further verbal acrobatics, Manuel got her to tell him her address. And there he is, just about to ring the bell. With no surprise to offer, no more acrobatics, only his hangover and a question.

"Last night?" Esther looks at him in bewilderment. "Nothing happened last night."

She's wearing cotton pyjamas with little teddy bears on them. She's holding a coffee cup in one hand. Behind her is another girl, possibly the one called Dayana. She's rather plump. She's fresh from the shower, and her hair is wet. There are others too. A group of girls up from the provinces, sharing an apartment. Esther and Mariana tell him everything was fine. "You gave us a lift back here in the early hours." He dropped them off outside, waited for them to go in and then left. Doesn't he remember?

And yet he feels no great relief. He's still not convinced. There's still no explanation for that piece of cloth sticking to his bumper.

He takes the metro back home. Being in the city's basement brings him some solace. He's had enough of streets. He knows he's at fault, that he has a debt. When he arrives back at his apartment building, he finds a neighbour engaged in washing his own vast blue estate car, last year's model. It's standing right in the middle of the courtyard covered in soap, like some huge beast. Manuel and the neighbour wave to each other from a distance. For a moment, he catches a glimmer of suspicion in his neighbour's eyes. As if the neighbour knew what was going on. As if he understood his anxieties. Perhaps, earlier on, he saw the piece of cloth stuck to the bumper. Everyone's seen the tracks you've left, Manuel.

He spends the afternoon engaged on the same search. With an ever deeper sense of desperation. He listens to the radio, waiting for a news item describing some fatal and inexplicable event that occurred in the early hours; he makes several inopportune phone calls to female friends or acquaintances, trying to find out if, by any chance, he turned up at their apartment last night, very late, or did something wrong which, unfortunately, he can't remember. He goes through his wallet far too many times, checks his bank balance, the clothes he was wearing. Nothing. Perhaps nothing happened. Perhaps all his fears are just part of some twisted fiction, the hidden side of a very bad hangover. Perhaps that piece of cloth doesn't even come from a pair of trousers. Perhaps someone merely happened to brush past. Imagination is always more authentic than reality. That's why it's sometimes so difficult to choose between the two.

By six o'clock, he's exhausted. A ray of sunlight comes in through the window and gently warms his legs. He groans and shifts restlessly in his sleep. He dreams that he's waking up from a nap with a terrible thirst. He's not wearing a shirt, but he does have his shoes on. He goes to the fridge, opens it and stands there, paralysed. Inside, lit by the bland glow of the refrigerator light, are several transparent plastic bags. These contain various human body parts. On the bottom shelf, in a small bag, he sees the blackened sole of a foot. In another bag, next to it, there are some fingers protruding from amongst certain dark, bulbous, irregular shapes in which he can almost make out a kidney or a piece of intestine. Manuel retches. He slams the fridge door. He bends double, but manages not to throw up. His feelings of nausea seem to have stopped him from fainting. His face, a distorted reflection in the silver door, looks blue now. He takes a deep breath. He closes his eyes. He takes another breath. It can't be true. It must be a dream. He opens the door again: on the top shelf, in a larger bag, is the homeless man's head. Lips open, eyes staring. The grime transformed into frost. The plastic is covered with small stains, like dark moles. As if the man had just coughed inside the bag.

Manuel wakes abruptly. He sits bolt upright, screaming. It takes a few seconds for him to separate himself from those images. He's terribly thirsty. He finds it hard to breathe. On automatic pilot, he goes to the kitchen, arrives at the fridge, and when his hand touches the door, he stops dead. He looks at his face reflected in the silver body of the fridge. He doesn't dare enter his dream.

By ten o'clock, he is thoroughly fed up with himself. He can't bear
this restlessness, this invisible, disembodied guilt. Determined to
resolve the matter once and for all, he goes down to the car park,
gets into his car and leaves. He wishes his car could drive itself,
naturally guiding him to the place where either imagination or
vodka have constructed a street.

On a corner of Avenida Libertador, he sees various transvestites got up in brightly coloured dresses with sequinned
necklines. He lights his first cigarette of the day. The smoke
scratches his throat. A car has stopped at the lights. There are
several men inside. They are talking loudly and laughing. One of
the transvestites goes over to them. The lights change and Manuel
drives on. He's still heading for the centre, but when he reaches
Avenida Universidad, he turns round, intending to go back.
Just then, on that bend, he sees him. Or thinks he does. Perhaps
he only senses his presence, his shadow. A bent, narrow figure,
carrying a bag. A stunted creature with a crest of rubbish on its
back. Manuel stops the car. He screws up his eyes, trying to fix the
image. In the distance, he hears a siren. For a second, he remembers those transvestites. The men have got out of the car. They're
all hopelessly drunk. One of them takes out a pistol and waves
it in the air, as if he were shaking his penis after peeing. One of
the transvestites smashes a beer bottle on a lamp post, transform-
ing it into a knife. Manuel gets out of his old Fiat. He leaves the
lights on, illuminating the dark corner where he thinks he saw the
homeless man. He approaches, feeling tense and nervous. It's a

corner piled high with rubbish bags. It smells rotten, it smells of shit. The man is there, crouched down, rummaging around for tin cans. The police siren is still going. There are shots as well. The man turns and sees Manuel. Startled, he draws back. Manuel does the same. The man shuffles backwards on his bottom, keeping his eyes fixed on Manuel. He mutters something that Manuel can't understand.

"Wait," Manuel says fearfully, with more despair than conviction, but nonetheless taking a step forward.

The man leaps over various bags, sinks into them, almost falls, jumps up again, stumbles, and finally makes it onto the street. He starts to run. Feeling ever more bewildered, Manuel hurries back to his car, turns on the engine, and goes after him. He can't hear anything now. No shots, no sirens. On the corner where he saw the transvestites, there is only broken glass on the ground. Manuel is driving slowly down the middle of the avenue, looking from side to side. The headlights suddenly illuminate the ungainly figure of the homeless man. He's running barefoot over the tarmac. Manuel puts his headlights on full. A breath of white light envelops the fleeing man. There is no difference between his ragged clothes and his skin. Everything is grime, dirt. Manuel drives on, sees him stumbling and limping ahead of him, getting ever closer. It must be a dream. This can't be happening. Manuel just wants to wake up. He closes his eyes and slams his foot down on the accelerator.

Why Don't Women Like Porn Movies?

The story could begin with Adriana peering through the half-open door and seeing the naked man. He's lying on the bed. His horribly swollen penis lies, drooping and defeated, on the sheets. Adriana suddenly feels something akin to vertigo. That's how it should begin, but, in fact, the story starts a few days before. Not in that room. Not in that fifth-floor room. Not with that man, but with her husband, a detail that possibly doesn't really matter now, given that all men are bastards. Without exception. Even those men who appear not to be. Give them a chance and you'll see, they won't let you down. It's written in the most ancient of alphabets, in a language unknown to the male deities. All men are bastards. Prepare yourself. Sooner or later, they'll make you suffer. There's no escape.

The phone rings at 2.00 in the morning. Adriana wakes with a start. She glances across at the other side of the bed. Rodrigo is still not home. He went to play dominoes with some friends. I won't be back until late, he said. The phone rings again. What kind of time is this to be ringing? Why so late? The phone is still ringing. Adriana hears Pablo stirring in his room. She's afraid he might pick up the phone. Finally, she grabs the handset herself and, finally, says a tremulous hello.

Visiting a public hospital is like visiting a street full of pedlars and street vendors displaying their personal misfortunes. Adriana doesn't like this image, but there it is: it surrounds her, wraps about her. She'd like to shoo it away as if it were a fly. The image, unfortunately, is not an insect and won't be shooed away so easily. Adriana pushes through the crowd. She's passed by a man on a stretcher with multiple stab-wounds to his stomach. Adriana feels sick. What do human guts smell like? She tries to talk to a doctor: They told me my husband was here, she says anxiously. His name is Rodrigo Ugarte, and he's had an accident. Another wounded man passes. A patient passes by, pushing a mobile IV drip from which dangle a saline bag and a catheter. A nurse passes pushing a wheelchair. A bloodstain passes. The smell of ammonia passes. In the midst of all this chaos, the doctor vanishes. Half an hour later, he returns: Who was it asking for Ugarte? he shouts. He's been transferred to another hospital, because the intensive care unit here has had to close, he announces, before turning and disappearing for good. Adriana leaves as fast as she can. She can't wait to escape from this street market. Everything smells bad to her, it smells of people about to die.

There are fewer people at the university hospital, which always helps. The police think her husband was resisting an attack. That's why he's in a coma. There were two shots: the first entered his jaw and exited through the right side of his face; the second entered his back and must have collided with something or other, because it didn't come out again. Adriana feels almost as if they were talking about a particularly capricious bullet. Some bullets are like that. They decide to lodge in a body, to inhabit it. Like visitors who arrive and stay and never say goodbye. Never leave.

That's all she's been told. In the brief newspaper item describing the incident, the journalist also appears to think it was a mugging. No-one knows precisely what happened. And Rodrigo can't explain. He can't even breathe without help. He's plugged into a series of machines that keep him alive, if you can call it that. He is alive, but only just.

After two days, she has at last been allowed to see him. The intensive care ward is quite small, with one large window that looks out onto a corridor. Adriana and Pablo observe Rodrigo through this window. There are three other patients with him: a very fat old lady and, beyond her, another two indistinguishable bodies. They can see only the dark, bony feet of the first one; the second is just an irregular shape beneath a sheet. The boy sees his father through the glass panes. Adriana doesn't know what to say, she grasps Pablo's hand and they both stand there in silence, looking. As if Rodrigo were swimming around in a fishbowl.

At the weekend, Pablo goes to stay with his grandparents while Adriana remains at the hospital. She doesn't know what to do. She feels powerless. She doesn't understand what the doctors tell her. Her husband's life has suddenly become a string of incomprehensible words that always arrive at the same conclusion: no firm diagnosis, anything could happen, so be prepared. And yet, on Sunday morning, something happens for which she is not in the least prepared. Adriana finds another woman gazing into the intensive care ward. A young woman, less than thirty. She's thin and appears sad and distraught. Adriana is immediately touched. She looks at her with the knowing compassion only to be found among those sharing a hospital corridor. At first, Adriana assumes she must have come to visit the fat woman or is related to one of the other two bodies further off, but as the young woman approaches, and Adriana sees her eyes and the way she's looking at her, she realises this is not the case.

"Look, I hate having to say this to you in these circumstances," the woman says, coming over to her, "but you must be Adriana."

Adriana looks at her, surprised. The woman's eyes are red from crying. She seems very agitated.

"I'm Gledys," she says after a pause, "Rodrigo's girlfriend."

The two women look at each other. Adriana doesn't know how to react, what to say. Perhaps she needs a rerun of the whole thing. Yes, that would be perfect. A tearful girl comes over to her, looks at her, tells her: I'm Gledys, your husband's girlfriend. No. She doesn't say "husband". She says: Rodrigo's girlfriend. That is doubtless more familiar, more natural, more personal. She doesn't say "lover" either. She says "girlfriend". That's different. It sounds less sinful, less serious, less treacherous. Anyway, at moments like these, there's no room for jealousy. Or is there? On the other side of the glass, Rodrigo lies motionless, still breathing, but oblivious to everything. On this side of the glass, the two women look at each other again. Gledys's eyes are really very red. As if her tears burned.

Adriana's sister says:

"God, you're a fool! The biggest fool in the world! If I'd been there, I would have knocked her teeth out! Who does she think she is, the slut!"

Adriana says nothing. Her expression is still one of utter bewilderment. She'd had no idea what to say to the girl, how to respond. She was furious, of course. Hurt too. And humiliated as well, but it all seemed so absurd. What could she do?

"I hope you at least told her not to come back to the hospital."

"She did apologise for that, for having gone to the hospital, I mean. But she just couldn't stand it anymore, she said. She had to know what was happening."

"And I bet your husband was with her that night too. He certainly wasn't playing dominoes. He was rolling around in bed with that whore. Is she nice-looking?"

Adriana still doesn't know what to say. She wishes perhaps that she felt less confused. Meeting the girl has provoked all kinds of thoughts in her. For example, the fact that she hasn't cried. That from the moment she was told about the accident until now, she hasn't cried once. Certainly not like Gledys.

"And you didn't suspect a thing?"

"No, nothing."

"She's probably just a kid," her sister mutters after thinking for a few seconds.

"I reckon she's about twenty-six."

"Twenty-six! Well, bloody Rodrigo deserves exactly what he got!"

"Don't say that."

The sisters look at each other for a moment.

"All men are bastards."

That night, Adriana gets drunk. After putting Pablo to bed, she opens a bottle of wine and drinks. Men and women don't drink in the same way. Not even when both are basically aiming to get drunk. Women do it quietly, as if they were doing something else. As if "to drink" were not the main verb in the action, as if it were merely a melancholy substitute for another verb, describing a deeper, more important task. Adriana drinks now with that same fragility of purpose. It's almost as if she wasn't so much drinking as spending time with the wine. With no sense of urgency. Not so much possession as companionship.

Then she lies down on the bed and stares up at the ceiling lamp. She opens her legs, stretches them. She doesn't need a mirror to be able to see herself. She knows she's almost forty. She's at that strange biological halfway point. She's neither fat nor thin; she's neither athletic nor flabby; she doesn't look old, neither does she look young. That non-state suddenly strikes her as very cruel. When reaching out to take another sip of wine, she knocks over the glass, and the wine goes everywhere. A few days before, she would have leapt out of bed and changed the sheets. Now she continues thinking about her age, the almost forty that will become forty next August. She doesn't want to accept this as an explanation, a reason for Gledys to exist. She and Rodrigo have occasionally discussed the matter. They've talked seriously about routine, boredom, weariness. They've talked about sex and about their sex life. Does desire fade? They've talked about that too. It's the kind of thing all couples talk about when they've been together a long time. Often those conversations are only an attempt to postpone the inevitable: talking disguises things, talking dodges the issue, talking avoids being naked. Best to think of love as responsible and solid, whereas desire is frivolous and not to be trusted. Best not to linger too much over the details, but to conclude that it really doesn't matter, it's just a phase everyone goes through, that's how life is.

Once, Rodrigo brought home a pornographic movie. He didn't explain why, but he behaved as if this might get them in the mood. He was trying to create an atmosphere conducive to sex. They watched it together for a few minutes, but she became bored almost immediately. It all seemed so predictable to her, something for men to masturbate to. She couldn't see the point of the film at all. She found ogling other men's penises disagreeable in the extreme. Watching all that urgent sex was of no interest to her. It didn't excite her. He turned off the television. He felt frustrated, but also slightly ridiculous. Why don't women like porn movies? he asked. The question hung in the air for a moment between them. We used to go out to supper, go dancing, we used to talk, said Adriana, after a pause. There was an element of courtship, and courtship is very important. Now when you want to make love, you just plonk one hand on my tits and that's that. Those, more or less, were her words. Then a silence fell.

Adriana is again looking at Rodrigo through the glass. What should she feel? Anger? Hatred? Indignation? She doesn't feel any of those things. Should she perhaps wish to die? No, she really doesn't want that either. All she feels inside is a kind of opaque emptiness. That's all. A nurse comes over to her. The same one who was there the night her husband was admitted. She knows all about it, about Gledys and everything. Adriana doesn't like being so exposed; the nurse, on the other hand, behaves as if this were all perfectly normal. She says something along the lines of "all men are bastards", but uses different words, her own words. Then she tells Adriana about the man upstairs. He's well and truly fucked, she whispers suddenly.

The man upstairs is in room 508, on the fifth floor of the hospital. He has cancer of the penis, in the tip of his penis, in the glans. Nurses never stint on detail. She opens her hand and says:

"That's how big the tip of his cock is."

And then she goes on: it's the size of a baseball. Every morning, it's full of pus and maggots. A kind of disgusting, white grease. We clean it with anisette. Any sort will do, the kind you'd buy at an off-licence. Anisette kills the maggots, you see. But it really stings. He screams when we clean it. We remove the maggots with a pair of tweezers. They say he served time in prison for rape, and that's why he got cancer. But who knows? Anyway, no-one visits him. No-one's been to see him. It's a punishment from God, people say. He's being operated on tomorrow morning. They're going to cut off his cock. We couldn't be happier, the nurse says.

Adriana has spent nearly all afternoon sitting in the corridor, thinking or trying to think. While she's waiting for the doctor, Gledys arrives. She clearly finds the situation awkward too. You can't disguise embarrassment. Do you mind me coming here? she asks. She wants to be open about things. After all, they're both facing the same tragedy, both harbouring the same hopes. They're bound together by something more basic than an emotional dispute. They don't even know if tomorrow there will be a man to fight over, a body to share. But Adriana still doesn't know how to handle the situation. Perhaps she's afraid of losing her temper, flying off the handle, getting hysterical. Although perhaps that's what she needs to do. Why is she being so reasonable? Why is she choosing to suffer rather than explode? What are you supposed to do at times like these? What is the correct way to behave? She doesn't know. She agrees, or half-agrees, then leaves. She can't bring herself to confront the girl, to drive her away, nor is she capable of staying by her side. Being there with her is already an admission of defeat.

She sets off. She wanders around, trying to distract herself, not knowing what else to do. This is how she arrives at the fifth floor. By chance, unintentionally, simply killing time, letting herself be led by her feet. She walks past room 508. The door is ajar. When she passes, she sees a man lying on the bed. A glimpse. A silhouette that slips into one corner of her eye. But something makes her stop. Some strange inexplicable impulse. The story could have started here, with Adriana peering through the half-open door and seeing the naked man. He's lying on the bed. His horribly swollen penis lies, drooping and defeated, on the sheets. Adriana suddenly feels something akin to vertigo. The man slowly turns his head and looks at her. Her saliva grows thick and heavy. Perhaps she was expecting a different face. A crueller, more sinister expression. He's just another man.

She doesn't know what she's doing there, she doesn't understand why she's gone into that room. The man seems equally surprised. Perhaps he thinks she's got lost and has come into his room by mistake. Adriana cannot move. And yet, observing this naked man and his repellent body, she feels no disgust or anger. Rather, there's something painfully troubling about the whole scene. The man looks at her, as if asking for help. Or so she feels. His hollow eyes shift restlessly in their sockets. What are they asking for? Then she looks at his penis, his diseased and grubby penis. The man makes no effort to cover himself. He lies there, naked, looking at her. Doesn't he feel ashamed? She again looks him in the eye and sees there an indecipherable melancholy. Tomorrow he will be punished. Without taking his eyes off her, the man very slowly moves his hand towards his penis. Adriana goes cold. At no point do they say anything.

Then Adriana comes to her senses and realises she's standing there staring at the penis of a complete stranger. He's touching himself now. Their eyes are still locked together. Then, when she can bear it no longer, she abruptly leaves the room, every step she takes hammering inside her head, and goes back out into the corridor.

She just about manages to make it to a chair opposite the door of the room. A nurse comes over to her. Adriana is terribly pale. She feels sick too. She can no longer contain her feelings. She begins to cry. She does so undramatically, but loudly. As if she had never cried before in her life. A cleaner approaches her. As do two other curious onlookers. They talk about her to each other. The nurse goes into the room and comes back out. Adriana can't stop crying. She doesn't know how to.

"Do you know that patient?" The nurse crouches down in front of her, looks at her, concerned, and takes her hand. "Are you related to him in some way?"

The Open Veins

FOR RICARDO CAYUELA

We had been neighbours ever since we were kids. We lived in the same district, went to the same school, were in the same class, had the same teacher. His mother was younger than mine, so we were different in that respect. She must have been about forty. Or a bit less. They lived alone. Camilo's dad was always away travelling somewhere. At least that's what we all thought. Until the afternoon when a dark brown car drew up outside their house. Four men, armed but not in uniform, got out, knocked at the door, then kicked it in. They were looking for Camilo's dad. They turned the whole house upside down. They took papers, clothes, even a clock. Camilo's mum was called Belinda. She didn't say anything. She didn't cry or scream. She didn't even seem frightened. We all saw what was happening. The police questioned her, but she refused to answer. She seemed completely unfazed. Camilo was shaking though. He clung to her right leg and stared down at the ground. When the men had left, she offered no explanations. The neighbours all gathered round, some out of curiosity, others wanting to help. But she went back into her house, without so much as a good afternoon, without saying a word or turning round.

That night, I heard my parents talking quietly, near the window. "He's a guerrilla," my father said. "That's why they're looking for him."

This was towards the end of the 1970s. Camilo and I weren't yet ten years old. Some groups, survivors of the guerrilla adventure of the previous decade, were either still fighting a few last-ditch battles or trying, without too great a loss of dignity, to negotiate an amnesty and a return to civilian life. They succeeded in this a few years later. Six days before Camilo's fifteenth birthday, he and I met his father.

We were listening to salsa music in Camilo's room. In fact, I was trying to teach Camilo to dance. He was painfully shy and awkward. He had never learned to dance and didn't have much sense of rhythm. But the prospect of standing like a dummy in the middle of a party was simply too daunting. At the time, an inability to dance was generally viewed with great suspicion and seen as an unmistakable sign of affectation and a general lack of virility. Camilo made me swear not to tell anyone.

Sometimes, in the afternoons, we would shut ourselves up in his bedroom and start practising, with me as would-be teacher. "Watch carefully now, it's three steps," I was saying. *"Ta-tatá-ta.* Listen to the beat. That's it. Relax into it." We had a small cassette radio, which we played at full volume. I was a big fan of Ray Barretto. Especially his live version of *"El Guararey de Pastora"*. It featured two brilliant piano solos. Really cool it was. The afternoons were ideal because Camilo's mum worked as a seamstress in a clothes shop near the market. There was no-one else at home.

We sang and danced. Or rather we sang and tried to dance. *Pastorita tiene guararey conmigo / Yo no sé por qué será.* ("Pastorita's really angry with me, I don't know why.") That's what we were doing that afternoon when the door was suddenly flung open. We froze, our arms still around each other. It didn't make the best of impressions. In the doorway stood a small, grumpy-looking man. He was staring at us in bewilderment, as if he had no idea what to do next.

"Camilo?" he asked at last, in a slightly incredulous tone, looking from one to the other.

We separated and nodded, almost at the same time. As if we were both Camilo.

"Well, I'm your dad, dammit!" muttered the man.

Efrén Castañeda turned out to be far more normal than we expected. More commonplace, more ordinary. The first indication of this was his bald head. We were both astonished to find that he was bald. We'd seen the odd photo of Camilo's dad and in none of them did he appear like that, without a hair on his head. We were quite put out. For some unknown reason, we thought that a guerrilla could be anything, but not bald. We found his baldness completely unacceptable.

He had finally come back to practise politics legally, that is, from his own house, from the bosom of his family. Camilo's mother, however, was not at all pleased. Indeed, she seemed most upset about the return of the guerrilla. She was quite a lot younger than him, and quite a lot prettier too. Next to her, Camilo's father seemed smaller. Almost dumpy. He was definitely in urgent need of more height. It was equally difficult for us to accept that a guerrilla could be so utterly unimposing. In our view, he fell several inches short of the name "guerrilla". The worst of it, though, was the discovery that he was not in the least athletic. Once, while trying to straighten out one of the sheets on the corrugated roof, he fell off the ladder. It was a really difficult, unnerving moment. Camilo and I looked at each other, perplexed. His father, all too soon, had ceased to be a myth.

Ever since his arrival, Belinda had made him sleep in Camilo's room. There was nowhere else. The first defeat in this new war. Efrén Castañeda tried diverse strategies, attacked on various fronts, but always failed. It was clear that they were no longer a couple. Or even friends. It was clear, too, that all this rejection was deeply humiliating for his father. Every time his parents argued, Camilo would look away, stare down at his plate or simply leave the room. One Saturday, in front of us, Belinda yelled at him: "You and I are not husband and wife anymore." He had only been home for two weeks, but they had been arguing right from the start. They had done so discreetly at first, but gradually all attempt at concealment fell away. On another night, before going to sleep on the small camp bed in the corner of Camilo's room, his father gave a deep sigh and said:

"This is far worse than being a guerrilla up in the mountains."

Instead of spending our afternoons dancing, we began to spend them listening to him. This was important, especially for Camilo.

He had been waiting for his father for far too long. The legend finally had a body, a voice and stories to tell. But the version Efrén Castañeda gave of his experiences as a guerrilla was, frankly, disappointing. There was nothing heroic about it. He said things like: "When you're a guerrilla, you spend most of your time doing nothing. Sometimes, whole weeks can go by without you hearing a single shot. And I know what I'm talking about. I spent nearly fifteen years at it. All that stuff about Che is pure bunkum. Believe me, being a guerrilla is really boring. You have to know how to amuse yourself, because you have a lot of time on your hands."

We were beside ourselves with indignation. We found his words shameful. We were in the third year of secondary school and both of us belonged to a cell of the Popular Struggle Movement, a radical left-wing party. Within the group, thanks to his father's legacy, Camilo was almost a hero. I shared in a little of that glory too. We both basked in the special aura emanating from "Comandante Jerónimo" – Efrén Castañeda's *nom de guerre*. For our classmates, being able to share one's home with an ex-guerrilla was an achievement in itself. They were green with envy. And yet we couldn't possibly allow anyone near him let alone allow anyone else to meet him. We felt obliged to continue feeding the legend, to invent a father who bore less and less resemblance to Camilo's actual father. We added a few inches to his height and a little more bravado to his stories. We found a thousand ways of preventing him from leaving the house. In the afternoons, we would take advantage of his liking for rum and, while he talked, we would keep refilling his glass until sleep overcame him, and then we would pray that he slept until noon the next day. Again, Camilo made me swear not to tell anyone the truth, not to let anyone know what a complete arsehole his father was. Those were his exact words. I said yes. I swore. There was no mention now of congas. No *Pastorita* and no *guararey*.

The situation in Camilo's house rapidly deteriorated. His father did nothing. He ate, drank, slept, existed. Like a stranger, like a tenant who can never be evicted, however badly he behaves. The confrontations between him and Belinda became more frequent and more heated. They were either screaming at each other or refusing to speak. She avoided him as much as possible, and did everything she could not to have to talk to him or see him. She would arrive home late and lock herself in her room. Efrén would go looking for her and knock on her door. Depending on how much rum he'd drunk, he would either speak softly or shout or even howl, railing against her, accusing her of betraying him, of having another man, of deceiving him; or he might just sit on the floor, like a child, his head pressed to the door, whimpering, moaning, begging forgiveness, pleading with her to open up, not to reject him, to give him a little love. "Just a kiss. Is that too much to ask, Belinda?" Yes, he had sunk that low.

Camilo would listen from his room, cringing with embarrassment. Sometimes he would turn up the volume on the television and then, when his father finally slouched in, he would almost invariably pretend to be asleep.

*

"I remember once, we were marching in the foothills of Villa-nueva. There were quite a few of us. More than fifty. We were in the middle of nowhere. The people in charge of security assured us that the army was no longer in the area. They gave us the day off. I'm not kidding. Even guerrillas get days off now and then. It was a really big deal. We could actually shout if we wanted. Do you know what it's like being given permission to shout after spending weeks on the alert, on guard, hiding away and taking care not to make any noise at all? For some time, we'd been holed up, almost trapped, but had finally managed to escape. After walking for days and days, it seemed we were safe at last. And then we were told: you can shout, you can sing. Even if that permission only lasted a few hours. I mean it. It was like a party. What did we sing? Can't you guess? No, you can't. It was in 1971 more or less, around about then anyway. We had received two presents. I remember it like it was yesterday. A new book, *The Open Veins of Latin America* by Eduardo Galeano, and a cassette that had also come out that same year. It was by Juan Gabriel, his first record. We'd already heard some of the songs on the radio, which we were usually allowed to listen to in the early morning. And so that's what we did. We sat in the sun. About fifty unwashed, heavily bearded guys, rifles on our backs, all of us deep-dyed communists and guerrillas, singing: *No tengo dinero, ni nada que dar* "*Lo único que tengo es amor para dar.*" ("I have no money or anything else to give, all I have is love.")

Efrén Castañeda creased up laughing at the memory of that afternoon. His eyes filled with tears too. Tears of laughter. We sat there in silence, amazed, not knowing quite what to do with this anecdote, while he poured himself another drink. "We were like a load of poofters," he said, standing up and wiggling his hips in a poovy manner, reliving the moment. "Poofs in olive-green fatigues," he said, before singing that same chorus again.

Several months passed, and day-to-day life in Camilo's house grew steadily worse. His father and another group of ex-guerrillas put themselves forward as congressmen, but without success. None of them gained the necessary number of votes to enter the National Congress, which was hardly surprising, since none of them held any political post of any kind. They were virtual unknowns. They belonged to a different world, they were merely a failed subplot in history. They began to realise that the dream of "reintegration into the social and political life of the country" would take effort, patience and luck. Efrén Castañeda didn't even have a job, a way of financing himself. He lived on the generosity of a few comrades or ex-comrades and, from time to time, wrote overly complicated articles for small journals that paid very badly and which no-one read. He was out of step with the times. He had returned to a country he didn't know. He had no future, and his past was looking increasingly dubious.

Belinda tried several times to throw him out of the house, but he invoked his rights as owner: the house belonged to him, he had bought it. This was true. He was right. Fate plays these tricks sometimes: Comandante Jerónimo saved by private property.

Camilo was equally fed up. Belinda and he stopped giving

Efrén any money, skimped on food, and generally made their disapproval felt. But Efrén Castañeda withstood all this with blithe indifference. What Camilo found most surprising was his father's ability to sleep. He could sleep anywhere, in any circumstances, whenever he chose. For his father, sleeping was an act of will. He slept when he decided to. One afternoon, he told us that he could even control his unconscious mind, that he could manipulate his dreams. During his years as a guerrilla, he had developed a method that allowed him to choose what he dreamed each night. "It's not an exact science, of course. But I did manage to pinpoint certain areas, certain general themes." Before heading off into the mountains, Efrén Castañeda had studied psychology at the Central University. He didn't get beyond the third semester – "my political activism took up all my time" – but he did dip into certain books by Freud, especially *The Interpretation of Dreams*. "That was the one that interested me most." When, as a guerrilla, he had nothing to do, "which, as I told you, happened a lot", he spent his time thinking about what he had read. "I would use my imagination to amuse myself." He even invented a fictitious character, a doctor, "another Jew", who lived in Vienna at the same time as Freud. "A similar sort of man, but different, if you know what I mean." He gave him a name: David Singer. "That was the name of a Jew I met in Maracay, when I was a boy." In Efrén Castañeda's imagination, Singer was a noted doctor, a nutritionist, who, like Freud, believed that dreams had a purpose, "that they were a symptom, that they expressed something that was going on inside the body". Which is why, given his own academic specialism, he developed a whole theory about the influence of food on dreams. After many years of research, he managed to establish a relationship between various nutrients and certain variables in our apparently random nocturnal fantasies. "Isn't that amazing?"

Making creative use of their idle hours, Singer and Castañeda devoted themselves to experimenting with different types of protein and carbohydrate, different fats and calories. "We used whatever we had to hand, not that there was much to choose from up in the mountains." As best they could, given the unpredictable nature of a guerrilla war, they continued to develop their theory. Any experiment was valid. "I tried eating stones, sand, monkey shit, anything." In this way, they began to draw up a probable map, a system of laws which, slowly, led to the creation of "the Singer method of dream production". It was a proven system. "Quite extraordinary." According to Efrén, depending on what an individual ate, the unconscious mind would always produce the same results. "The connection between carrots and sexual fantasies is a no-brainer. It never fails. Try it."

As time passed, Efrén wearied of Singer and killed him off. "He was basically a failure. That's how I imagined him anyway, as a loser." A luckless Jew. His studies were never recognised. He never even got to meet Freud face to face. His fate resembled a bad film script. Singer couldn't even escape the Nazis. He died, in Castañeda's version of events, in a death camp in 1941. "The same way they screwed a lot of people: gassed to death with pesticide."

*

After that conversation, Camilo and I went for a walk. Camilo was at the end of his tether. He was finding his father ever harder to bear. He felt that he couldn't stand him for another second. Imagining Comandante Jerónimo, in the middle of the guerrilla war, inventing that unlikely Jew intent on substituting the unconscious mind with the body's gastric juices: this seemed to him a step too far. "We all imagined such stories. We had to amuse ourselves somehow." It no longer just depressed him listening to his father talk, it now provoked an inner fury, a seething, dyspeptic rage that began in the pit of his stomach and rose unstoppably up into his mouth. He was afraid he might, at any moment, lose control.

And that is precisely what happened that same night. We walked around the streets for a while, had a few beers, and he arrived home late, at about eleven o'clock. His mother, as usual, was locked in her room. Through the door, he could hear the sound of the radio, although he couldn't identify the music. It was a strange, gentle music, wind instruments, but which he nevertheless found unrecognisable. Music from a country whose name he doubtless didn't even know. He was about to knock, but thought his mother might think Efrén Castañeda was once again spying on her through the keyhole, begging for a little compassion. He decided instead to go to his room. There he found his father asleep on the camp bed. He hadn't even taken off his shoes. He was lying on his back, shirtless, his arms flung wide. Camilo approached the bed and regarded his father with a certain degree of scorn. He bent over him and carefully observed his half-open lips, his closed eyes, his broad brow, his bald head. Were he and his father alike? Did they actually resemble each other? And if so, in what way? At the time, he rejected any possible resemblance between himself and that man, who, only a few months before, had introduced himself as his father. He bent still closer. He could smell his father's thick breath, a mixture of rum and foul air. He felt disgusted.

"What are you dreaming about now, you bastard?" he muttered.

His father continued his regular breathing, as if impervious to those words. As if, at that moment, nothing could touch him. Camilo felt like shaking him, like kicking him while he slept.

"You know what? You disgust me. I feel no pity, no sadness. You just disgust me, you prick," he whispered. And he said this angrily, but also sadly.

His father's body remained motionless. Camilo's words were like so much fruit peel falling limply onto the floor. Useless.

Camilo lay down on his own bed, also on his back. He closed his eyes for a moment. He had never felt so powerless. If he could plan his dream, what would he choose? What would he want to dream about just then, that night?

He imagined a dream in which he killed his father.

He immediately opened his eyes wide in fright. Efrén Castañeda was still there, unchanged. In dreams, no-one stays dead. He closed his eyes again, then heard these words:

"My sentiments exactly."

Camilo sat up, as if the bed had kicked him.

"No, really, I feel just the same."

His father hadn't moved.

"Were you awake?" Camilo managed to stammer out.

His father didn't reply. The question was too ridiculous, the answer too obvious. Camilo fell back, then slowly sat up again in bed, waiting. How many minutes did they sit there in silence? It's hard to say. Not all time can be measured by clocks. Camilo was suddenly afraid that his father really had now fallen asleep, that he had chosen a dream and fled into it. He suddenly remembered David Singer, the loser, the luckless Jew, who had come so close to being touched by history. Failure knows no shame.

Camilo decided to speak, even though his father had still not moved, his eyes tight shut, his mouth half-open. He didn't want to leave that conversation unfinished. He preferred to take a risk. He told his father that he was ashamed of him, that he had lost all respect for him, that his guerrilla life, his whole life as Comandante Jerónimo, seemed to him now a complete farce, a folly, a lot of ridiculous nonsense. He said he was sick of sleeping in the same room as him. He said he didn't want to see him again. "Who the hell gave you the right to think you were my father?" he said.

Efrán Castañeda continued sleeping. Or not. Camilo couldn't tell. He waited a while, then turned out the light.

When he woke the following morning, his father had packed up all his things and put them in a cardboard box. He was wearing a white shirt. It was an old shirt, but clean. He had also washed and shaved. He was sitting on the camp bed, as if he had been there for a while, waiting for Camilo to wake up. His father got straight to the point:

"Before I go, I want to tell you a story, one of those stories you so enjoy."

Camilo didn't even have time to go to the toilet. He heard him out, despite an urgent need to pee and despite the bitter taste of night on his tongue. "It happened somewhere about forty miles to the east of Humocaro Bajo. We were a company of ten men, and we had pretty much had it. We were trying to escape to the foothills of the Andes. The local villagers had betrayed us to the army." Efrén spoke with a seriousness he had never shown his son before. His company was broken and debilitated. Ailing and trapped. "We weren't far from the spot where we'd arranged to meet up with other troops who could, in theory, help us. And just at that point, we came to a clearing and saw a hut. In the middle of nowhere, in the mountains." It was a small adobe hut with an earthen floor. Outside, next to some banana trees, a fire was burning. A thread of smoke rose slowly up and disappeared among the tallest branches of the trees. "We all froze. We couldn't afford to stop. We knew we were being followed. Only two nights before, there'd been an exchange of rifle-fire with the army." The men looked at each other. It was only a second. The second it takes to exchange looks and for guns to wake up and prepare themselves to kill.

A woman appeared at the door of the hut. "She was a very thin young woman." Her skin was brown from the sun, her hair long and dark. She was wearing an old ochre-yellow dress that came

148

down below her knees. She was carrying a child in her arms. "Two or three years old. Almost naked." Everything smelled of damp wood and rotting leaves. The child clung to the woman's neck. "We asked if there was anyone else in the house. She didn't answer." She just shook her head vaguely, hesitantly. She was frightened. "We couldn't leave her there. That's what Moncho our commander said." They argued among themselves. They couldn't agree. But they didn't have much time either, an army patrol might already be closing in on them and they couldn't risk trusting the woman to say nothing. "Only two weeks before, a farmer from San Isidro had led us into a trap. We lost six men because of him." They couldn't trust anyone. The army had threatened all the people living in the area. The woman went over to the fire. She stirred the logs with a metal rod and blew on the flames. Then she looked at them. "Moncho talked about sacrifice, said we were at war and other such nonsense. But he chose me."

His father got up. As if he had been chosen right there and then, as if he were reliving that moment. He took a few paces about the room. He drew three circles in the air with his hand. Camilo followed him with his eyes.

"The others all headed up into the mountains, along a different path from the one we'd been following until then." Castañeda stayed behind. With orders to kill mother and child and then continue along the main path, as a decoy, to try and throw the army off their trail. "They left me alone with just a rucksack. We agreed to meet at nightfall at a place about six miles further east. The woman put the child down on the ground and looked at me hard, as if she already knew, you see, as if she knew what I had to do." Suddenly, a chicken appeared from behind the hut. The boy, barefoot, began chasing it. He ran after the bird, laughing. The woman walked over to Efrén. There was no fear in her eyes, only rage. A dumb, infinite rage. The boy's laughter spun around them. The woman made a gesture, but said nothing. Not a word. She just stared at him. "Those eyes. I've never seen anything so chilling."

He sat down again on the camp bed. He leaned one elbow on his knee and rested his cheek on his closed fist. He didn't say a word, he just looked at his son. Camilo lowered his gaze. For the first time, he felt really uncomfortable in his father's presence.

"What did you do?" Camilo asked.

"Do you know what I had in my rucksack?" his father said after a pause. "That bloody book by Galeano, the one about the open veins."

There was another silence. Then Efrén Castañeda started singing softly, without looking at Camilo:

"No tengo dinero, ni nada que dar / Lo único que tengo es amor para dar."

His father left that same morning, with the cardboard box under his arm, but walking proudly, head up. The days passed and he didn't come back. He didn't even phone. Camilo seemed quite unaffected. He even came to believe that the story about the woman and the child was an invention, another of his father's dreams, the dream chosen by Dr Singer and Comandante Jerónimo, the heroic lie with which his father wanted to mark his farewell. Camilo preferred not to talk about it.

It was nearly 6.00 on a Tuesday evening. Camilo had been intending to talk to Belinda ever since his father left. "My mother and me really need to have a chat about all this, about everything that's happened." That same day he decided they should have supper together and have that urgent talk. He went to pick her up from work. The shop was empty. Camilo walked through to the back, to the small room that served as a workshop, where his mother usually did her sewing. He couldn't hear the noise of the machine. He saw them as soon as he went in. Belinda and Fredy. Squeezed up in a corner, furiously touching and kissing each other. Fredy had his flies open. His cock was sticking out, erect, hard, and in the firm grip of Belinda's hand. We all knew Fredy. He was a local kid, like Camilo, like me. He would have been two or three years older than us. He studied at the same school. He played basketball.

Camilo went mad. That's what he told me. "I don't know what happened. I just went crazy." He hurled himself at Fredy, grabbed him by the throat and banged his head against the wall. "I don't remember a thing. But I know that I hit him with everything I had. Knees, fists, I think I even bit his face." His mother was screaming. Fredy was screaming. Camilo was screaming too. They tried to stop him, to subdue him, but it was no use. He was too angry, too out of control. They both fell to the floor. Camilo kept hitting Fredy. He crouched over him and began punching him in the face. "At one point, I felt his face go soft. It was like plunging my hand into a bowl of soup."

*

When Camilo got to my house, he was deathly pale. His hands and clothes were covered in blood. He kept walking round and round in a circle, nervous, confused, dizzy, not making any sense. I gave him a drink of brandy. I led him into the bathroom, where he washed himself. I gave him a shirt. We hardly spoke. He quickly told me what had happened and then left. He went out into the yard and jumped over the wall at the rear of the house. The last I heard was the sound of his feet landing on the pavement on the other side. Then his footsteps running away. Before he left, he made me swear to say nothing to anyone.

I went straight over to the shop. A police patrol had already arrived. There were a lot of people looking, talking. Everyone had something to say, rumours were rife, buzzing about like insects. On one corner, standing slightly apart from everyone, was Camilo's mother. Alone. I went over to her. I didn't know quite what to do. Suddenly, I felt this was all part of a bad dream, an impossible dream. Everything smelled of damp leaves and rotting wood. The woman made a gesture, but said nothing. Not a word. She simply stared at me. I had never felt anything like it before. Those eyes.

Translator's Acknowledgements

I would like to thank Alberto Barrera Tyszka for answering my queries so patiently; and my thanks, as always, go to Annella McDermott and Ben Sherriff for all their help and advice.

ALBERTO BARERRA TYSZKA is a poet, novelist and journalist. Together with Cristina Marcano he wrote the bestselling and critically acclaimed *Hugo Chávez* (2007), the first biography of the late Venezuelan president. His novel *The Sickness* was shortlisted for the Independent Foreign Fiction Prize and was the winner of the Heralde Prize in its original Spanish edition.

MARGARET JULL COSTA has been a literary translator for nearly thirty years and has translated novels and short stories by such writers as Eça de Queiroz, Fernando Pessoa, José Saramago, Javier Marías and Bernardo Atxaga. In 2014 she was awarded an O.B.E. for services to literature.